THE BOY WHO LIVED WITH DRAGONS

Andy Shepherd

THE BOY WHO LIVED WITH DRAGONS

Illustrated by
Sara Ogilvie

YELLOW JACKET

YELLOW JACKET
an imprint of Little Bee Books

New York, NY
Text copyright © 2018 by Andy Shepherd
Illustrations copyright © 2018 by Sara Ogilvie
All rights reserved, including the right of reproduction
in whole or in part in any form.
Yellow Jacket and associated colophon are trademarks of
Little Bee Books.
Manufactured in China RRD 1120
Originally published in Great Britain in 2018 by Piccadilly Press,
an imprint of Bonnier Zaffre Ltd.
First U.S. Edition 2021
10 9 8 7 6 5 4 3 2 1
Library of Congress Cataloging-in-Publication Data is available
upon request.

ISBN 978-1-4998-1178-0
yellowjacketreads.com

For more information about special discounts on bulk purchases,
please contact Little Bee Books at sales@littlebeebooks.com.

For Ian, Ben and Jonas,
for always cheering me on

Welcome, all you dragon-seeking desperadoes!

I'm guessing you've picked this book up for one of two reasons.

Either:

You've been hearing about how we grow dragons and you want to get in on all that juicy, fire-breathing action.

In which case, you need to go find yourself one of these:

Or:

You've found yourself a dragon fruit tree already, hatched yourself a dragon, and now have no clue what to do next.

How do I know this? Because neither did we.

After I found the dragon fruit tree in Grandad's garden, and Flicker—that's my dragon—hatched out in my bedroom, things changed pretty quickly. Not just because it sort of affects how you look at the world—I mean, if you can find a dragon in your bedroom on an otherwise normal Sunday, what else is possible? But also because he wasn't the only one. Not after my best friends, Ted, Kat, and, Kai decided they wanted one, too.

But just like you would be, we were too busy getting ourselves dragons to really wonder what having a dragon would actually be like.

I bet it all sounds magical, doesn't it? Growing a dragon. And it totally is, don't get me wrong. But let me tell you, when the fire-breathing really kicks in and

2

you're getting singed every five seconds, it's like having a very unpredictable volcano in your pocket. Then it all starts to feel a bit less magical. Just something to bear in mind, my dragon devotees.

So get some oven mitts, be prepared to hide your ripped-up pants and, above all, listen up. Because I'm about to show you what living with dragons is really like.

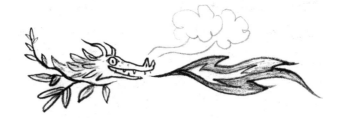

1
Solaris the Destroyer

"My underpants!" Ted cried as I opened the door. "Grab them!"

OK, I know it's not what you usually expect your best friend to say when you walk into their room, but listen, once you have a dragon, you need to be prepared for anything.

"I can't lose another pair out the window! That'll be the fourth in the last two days," he wailed.

I ducked as Sunny, Ted's golden dragon, swooped over my head. He'd crawled into Ted's underpants and was wearing them like battle armor. A fiery blast shot out and scorched the lampshade as the dragon circled above us. Flicker had been happily curled up in my pocket, but now he wriggled his way out. He hovered beside me while I tried to grab the underpants before they disappeared out of the open window.

"They better be clean," I wheezed, dropping them and coughing on the trails of smoke the dragon's breath had left behind.

"They were until he got in them," Ted moaned. "Now they're probably singed—or worse."

We both knew what he meant by worse. You see, dragon poop has this pretty unpleasant habit of exploding when it dries out. And sure enough, seconds later, Ted's underpants detonated spectacularly. Sunny zipped up to the top of the wardrobe while we stood there with foul-smelling shreds raining down on us.

"So, things going OK, then?" I grinned. "You know, among the exploding poop and being on twenty-four-hour Scorch Alert?"

Ted burst out laughing. "Well, that's Sunny for you."

Ted had actually named his dragon Solaris the Destroyer. I think he was imagining him as his superhero sidekick and wanted to give him a name that could conjure fear in all Ted's enemies. Or at least in Liam Sawston, who is our archnemesis. Not that we were about to share the secret of the dragons with him—we were spending most of our time trying to make sure that Nosy Nellie didn't find out about the dragons!

But let's face it, having a dragon called Solaris the Destroyer in your pocket kind of gave you the edge a bit. Anyway, Solaris the Destroyer only lasted a day because by his second morning, Ted had decided to call him Sunny. Officially, this is because Sunny is his dragon's alter ego, like Spider-Man is actually Peter Parker. But really—and this is just between us—it's because Ted is scared of the dark. And Sunny is the best night-light ever. The little dragon curls up next to him and glows, casting comforting orange light around the room. So Ted ended up feeling he was far too friendly for a name like Solaris the Destroyer. But like I said, that's just between us.

I was going to call my dragon Scorch after the first night I got him when he singed everything in sight. But the thing is, he changes color. He flickers. So Flicker just suited him. Most of the time he's red, although even then, he can't always decide what shade to be so he ends up shimmering through bright crimson all the way to deep ruby. When he's settling down to sleep on my sister Lolli's lap, his scales ripple turquoise, a colorful quiver of contentment. But if Tomtom, our cat, starts stalking him, he flares electric orange. The best thing is when I lie in bed with him curled up next to me and he starts glowing like a hot ember. And I fall asleep with him warming my dreams.

"Where've Kat and Kai got to?" Ted asked.

The twins, the other two members of our superhero squad, were always late, and so it was no surprise that they still hadn't appeared. In fact, now they had two dragons to contend with, they had the perfect excuse.

Ted's stomach gurgled like an angry drain and he grinned apologetically.

"What you mean is, 'Where have the snacks got to?'" I said.

"Well, yeah. Those, too. I can't keep anything edible in my room these days. Not when I leave Sunny in here on his own. Did you know a blue whale eats the equivalent of six thousand chocolate bars a day? Well, I reckon Sunny would have a good go at smashing that record if I let him try."

Flicker, who'd settled next to me, sneezed, sending

9

a glittering spray of sparks into the air. As usual—
thanks to my lightning reflexes—they were all snuffed
out before they'd even landed.

"Impressive," nodded Ted. "Sunny's less into the
nonstop sparking. He's more of a one-blast kind of
dragon. And he usually only does it when he's eaten.
Honestly, he has the most fiery farts. And talk about an
explosive burp!"

"But didn't you say he eats all the time?" I said,
looking round his room and realizing there was less
evidence of burning than you might expect.

"Yeah," Ted said with a shrug. "But mostly I can
tell it's coming and point the right end outside in time,
before he causes too much damage. That's why I have
to hide the snacks. If I know when he's eaten, I know
roughly when he's likely to blow up!"

It wasn't foolproof though—as we were about to
find out.

2
Into the Dragons' Den

When Kat and Kai pushed open Ted's bedroom door, they were met by a cascade of flaming wrappers. Sunny had clearly hidden a secret stash of goodies up on top of the closet and had been munching away as we waited. A fiery belch from him had set them alight and sent them flying.

Kai took the opportunity to bash Kat over the head with a rolled-up comic book. I'm not sure one of the burning scraps had even landed on her. I think it had more to do with the argument they'd obviously been having on the way over.

"No way. Dodger would beat Crystal, no question," he was saying, still brandishing the comic as his dragon, Dodger, wriggled out of his pocket and started zipping back and forth above us.

"As if," Kat replied, grabbing the comic away from him. She reached into her bag and lifted out her dragon. Crystal, with her bright purple scales swirling into electric blue, shook her head and the little spikes hanging like icicles under her jaws sparkled in the morning light. "Crystal's way faster. And anyway, she could ice her way to victory." And she whacked Kai on the arm with the comic for good measure.

"All right, you two," I said, jumping in before the disagreement could erupt like one of Sunny's belches. For all their "We stick up for each other, don't mess with my twin" thing, they argued a whole lot. It looked as if having a dragon didn't change things that much. If anything, it had just given them something else to compete over.

Ted was already unloading Kat's bag, pulling out

chips and ripping open chocolate bars and, stuffing them into his mouth whole.

"Good grief, Ted," laughed Kai. "You on starvation rations here or something?"

"Sorry, guys," Ted mumbled through another mouthful, wiping chocolate off his face. "You wouldn't believe how much Sunny eats! It's lucky Mom buys everything in bulk, but most of the snack supplies that are meant to last a month have been eaten in the last forty-eight hours. I had to restock it with my own stash. And I'm on thin ice anyway, thanks to Sunny using Mom's hatbox as a toilet and demolishing Dad's birthday cake. Mom still thinks that was me."

"Ew," grimaced Kat. "That's gross."

"Not the hatbox, the cake," Ted tutted. "Anyway, I can't risk him getting me into any more trouble."

"OK, so seriously, how is everyone getting along?" I asked.

One of the reasons we'd arranged to meet was to check how the dragons were settling in. It had been five days since the night where we had camped in Grandad's garden, crept down to the dragon fruit tree, and caught the dragons. And five days since the flaming fiasco of flying cabbages brought about by our other even grumpier nemesis, Grim, my Grandad's next-door neighbor and a man who made the Grinch look friendly.

Ted handed me a marshmallow, expertly toasted by Sunny.

"He's great at flame-grilling, although I wouldn't recommend jelly beans. I'm still getting those out of the carpet."

"And look at this," Kat said. She reached over to Ted's table and picked up a glass of orange juice. She held it in front of Crystal, who blew an icy breath across the surface of the drink. We all watched—and then flinched—as she attempted to throw the contents of the glass at us. But instead of splattering us, the orange juice stayed in the glass. Crystal had frozen it solid. Kat grinned.

"Thanks to Crystal, we'll have a never-ending supply of ice pops in the summer."

Ted's eyes lit up. He was probably imagining giant bucket-sized lemonade ice pops.

Obviously not wanting to be outdone, Kai jumped in.

"And Dodger is the best thief ever. Because he's like one of those chameleons, changing color to blend into his surroundings."

As if to prove the point, a family-size bag of popcorn rose up out of Kat's bag and flew towards Ted, narrowly avoiding bashing him in the face. Invisible against the blue quilt cover, none of us had even noticed Dodger sneaking towards the open bag.

Everyone looked at Flicker, now sitting quietly on my shoulder, his tail curled around my neck. Out of the corner of my eye, I saw the little pulse of turquoise ripple through his scales that meant he was settling in for another sleep.

I couldn't offer toasted marshmallows or ice pops, and Flicker couldn't camouflage himself and become a pickpocket like Dodger. Ted, Kat, and Kai were so excited about what their dragons could do—they all had something special to brag about. But flickering different colors didn't feel that useful. So I quickly changed the subject.

"Come on—let's take them out to the den," I said.

Ten minutes later, we all crawled into the hedge that ran along the edge of the park and through to the space we'd cleared inside it. It had always been a tight fit and more so since the dragons had arrived. But it was still a totally brilliant hideout. People walking their dogs strolled right past us and never knew we were there. Except when we got the giggles. But even when anyone peered into the undergrowth, they usually couldn't spot us.

I reached into my pocket and fished out a stalk of broccoli, feeding it to Flicker over my shoulder. A little pulse of heat warmed my neck as he happily chewed on it.

Ted had already found the perfect marshmallow-toasting stick and was busy threading a long line of pink-and-white gooey blobs onto it.

"You going for the world's largest s'more?" Kai asked, as Ted pulled out a packet of graham crackers.

"Largest snore?" I said, confused.

"No. s'more," Kai said. "You know, a graham cracker-and-marshmallow sandwich like they have round campfires in America."

Ted snorted. "I wish. Deer Run Camping Resort holds that record: two hundred sixty-six pounds!" Then he added, "That s'more was taller than me and more than twice as wide. Took a hundred and four people to make it." He gazed into the distance and gave a happy sigh.

I laughed. Trust fact-tastic Ted to actually know this.

"I've got an idea," said Kat.

We all watched as she held up a piece of bark in front of Crystal, who obligingly took a bite out of it. Kat moved the piece of bark and the dragon bit again. She did this over and over until she was left with a zigzag pattern down each side.

"Now, if I fasten this onto one of these bigger branches with a bit of melted marshmallow, can one of your dragons help out with a little fiery breath—and I mean a *little* fire?"

"Sunny's been feasting on marshmallows all the way here—he's due a fiery belch about now," said Ted. "Here you go."

Ted held his yellow dragon and pointed him towards the piece of bark.

Sure enough, Sunny started glowing golden and the next second, a fiery blast scorched the branch. Kat waited for the heat to die down and then grabbed the blackened bark, peeling it off.

There in front of us was a spiky-edged emblem emblazoned on the wood.

"Cool!" Kai said. "I want a turn."

By the time we had finished, each of us had marked a corner of the den with our own dragon-chomped design. I'd tried for a star shape, which might have been a little ambitious. Still, I was pretty pleased with the wonky, three-pronged sort of star that Flicker had nibbled for me.

"This place looks awesome," Kai said.

"Welcome to the Dragons' Den," Kat said with a grin.

3
S'mores Galore

Over the next few days, anytime we weren't at school or sleeping, we met at the Dragons' Den.

"We're going to need our own recipe book at this rate," Kai said when I crawled through the gap to find the others one afternoon. He was sitting surrounded by all sorts of packets of cookies and marshmallows, ranging from the tiny ones you stick in your hot chocolate to giant, fist-sized ones. Plus a mixture of sweets—and wrappers, thanks to Ted and Kat happily chewing their way through handfuls of them. "We can call it S'mores Galore!" he added.

It was true that we'd come up with some pretty awesome customized s'mores. My personal favorite was a gingersnap and chocolate wafer combo with jelly beans sandwiched into the center of the marshmallow.

"Anyone for another slushy to wash it down?" Kat asked, waving a large cup at me.

"Thanks," I said, taking an enormous slurp. "Hide and seek?" I asked, turning to the others.

They groaned. "You mean so you can beat us again and smash your record to find us all in under ten seconds?" Ted asked.

I grinned. It was true that currently the score was twenty-six finds to me, zero to anyone else. Flicker might not have the skills of the other dragons when it came to freezing, toasting, and camouflage, but he was the best seeker ever. With him on my side, I couldn't lose. Every time his diamond eyes spotted one of the others, he hovered next to their hiding place and flickered like a beacon, leading me right to them.

Just as Ted shoved another s'more into his mouth, Kat grabbed my arm and put a finger to her lips. We all sat as still and silent as we could, Ted doing a brilliant impression of Horatio the Hamster, Mr. Firth's class pet—an animal who believed there was no limit to what he could cram into his cheeks.

Kat edged closer to the gap in the hedge, peered through, and then quickly pulled across the branches we used to cover the entrance.

"It's Liam," she hissed. "He's coming this way."

I looked around at the dragons perched on the branches above us and kicked myself for not being more careful. What if he'd seen us disappearing into the hedge and was out to discover our den? What if he'd seen the dragons?

None of us dared breathe. In fact, I was starting to wonder if Ted actually could breathe with his mouth so full. His eyes were beginning to bulge. I could hear Liam's footsteps getting closer and it sounded as if he was muttering to himself. He was only a few feet away now. Branches started shaking. He was kicking the hedge or bashing it with a stick. I had images of a sharp spear jabbing into our den and poking us till we squealed. I wouldn't have been surprised if he could hear my heart, thumping away like a drum signaling our position.

Flicker flitted down and settled on my shoulder. His tail batted to and fro and I could feel the heat from his little body. He was getting hotter and hotter. Either he was as agitated as I was or he was, about to unleash a fiery sneeze.

But then suddenly, instead of edging closer to where we were all crouched and carrying on his investigation, Liam yelped like he'd been stung and we heard his footsteps crashing away in the other direction. I let out my breath in a relieved whimper and sank back onto the ground. Flicker nibbled my ear and wrapped his tail around my neck, as his scales, which had flared orange, returned to their familiar red.

"Ha! Serves him right," Kat said. "Bet those nasty stinging nettles zapped him."

Ted's cheeks deflated as a barrage of s'more splattered out of his mouth. "That was too close," he wheezed.

I nodded. If Liam, "King of Trouble" ever found out about the dragons—well, I didn't want to think about what might happen.

"You know, maybe we shouldn't take the dragons to school tomorrow?" I said.

It was something we'd been talking about for the past couple of days. Flicker had always been quite happy to curl up in my room and wait for me to come home. I missed him of course, and there was always a certain amount of damage to clear up, but with Liam's beady eyes locked on me, it had felt like the safest option. The others wanted to keep their dragons with them all the time, though. And I didn't like the idea of being the only one of us without my dragon. But seeing Liam again made me wonder if we should risk it.

"I think we're better off keeping them with us," Ted said.

"Yeah, come on, Tomas, they'll be fine," Kai said. "I'm not letting Liam spoil things. What could go wrong?"

As it turned out—quite a lot.

4
Attack of the Mutant Pigeon

By the time we got to school the next day—and after a lot of debate—we'd decided to stash the dragons in our backpacks in the walk-in art closet just off the main hall. First in through the school gates, we flashed Mrs. Muddleton, our head teacher, our widest, most innocent, "we're not really up to anything and are just here on time for once because we're super-excited to learn" faces. Of course, by the look on her face, she might not have picked up on all of that. But it was enough to make her cast her glance elsewhere and leave us to duck in through the door to the hall, rather than carry on towards our classroom.

Checking there was no one around to see, Kat pulled the closet door open and we all stared in. It was a bit of a mess, chock-full of paint trays and brushes

and crates full of cardboard for junk modeling. We made a space near the back, behind some boxes full of mini cereal boxes, then put some huge art folders and a box robot made by the kindergartners in front of the backpacks.

"Come on, Tomas," Kat said, as I lingered by my bag.

"Do you think they'll be OK in here?" I asked.

"Of course," Ted said. "I brought enough snacks to keep them all quiet for a week, let alone till lunchtime."

"You mean the snacks I saw you chomping your way through on the way to school?" laughed Kat.

Ted looked sheepish, but before I could check on the dragons' remaining supplies, Kai piped up.

"They'll be fine. But we won't be, if we're late for class. Come on, hurry up, you guys."

So whispering a reluctant farewell to Flicker, I followed the others out of the closet and hurried into class. I just hoped Liam's beady eyes were pointed in any direction other than at us today. And I hoped everyone was right and that the dragons would be OK until lunchtime, when we could take them down to the end of the field and let them out for a quick fly. If I'm honest, there seemed to be a lot of hoping going on. Hoping things wouldn't go wrong. Hoping we didn't get found out. Hoping we didn't run into trouble. But of course, run into trouble we did—smacked headlong into it, in fact. Because as it turned out, trouble was just around the corner.

It was a few minutes before lunch and we were late coming back from PE. Ted and I were hurrying to catch up with the rest of the class while Kat waited for Kai, hissing at him to get a move on. As we turned the corner to pass the staff room, we ran into Mrs. Fear—I know, great name for a teacher, right? She was actually one of the nicest, despite her name. She was talking to Mr. Woddle, the caretaker. Or she was until Ted bounced off her and landed in a heap on the floor.

"This is why we don't run, boys. Now hurry along to class."

We looked at her, waiting for her to fully realize what she'd just said and laugh or something. But she was completely unaware and returned her attention to the caretaker.

"But how would a duck get into the art closet, Mr. Woddle?"

"How should I know that? All I know is a duck has been dancing its way all over that closet. And it's a royal mess."

Mrs. Fear gave a little sigh.

"Right, let's have a look then, shall we?"

Kat and Kai had caught up with us just in time to hear the gist of the story. And as Mrs. Fear and Mr. Woddle headed off down the corridor, the four of us stared at each other in horror.

"One of them must have escaped and got into the paints," Kat gasped.

"I bet we can guess which one," I said.

Sunny was always hungry, and no doubt had decided he'd had enough of waiting for us to return with the next snack.

Kat suddenly gave a bloodcurdling shriek and started staggering down the corridor after Mrs. Fear and Mr. Woddle's retreating backs. Me, Ted, and Kai looked at her as if she'd gone completely bonkers, as the grown-ups spun round.

"Kat!" Mrs. Fear said, shocked. "Whatever has got into you?"

Now, Kat was quite the actress. She'd been lead in the school play for the last three years, and here's why. She could go from zero to "convincing hysteria" in about three seconds flat. She winked at us and we quickly realized what she was up to.

"Oh, miss, it was horrible," Kat wailed. She was only just managing to get her words out through huge gasping sobs. "I hate them, you see. I'm terrified of them."

"Of what?" Mrs. Fear said, as Kat clung to her arm. I was so impressed, I was even starting to worry for her myself until Ted kicked my foot and made a very obvious nodding movement for us to get away.

"Pigeons, miss." And here, Kat gave another drawn-out sob, accompanied by a dramatic shudder. "And this one flew right at me."

"A pigeon?"

"Yes, a pigeon. It attacked me. And I can't stand birds, I really can't. Oh, miss, it flapped right at my hair, and I'm sure it was chasing me. And it must have been some kind of mutant pigeon, because it had a purple head and yellow feathers. Is it still there? Can you see it?"

Mrs. Fear sighed, put her arm around the inconsolable Kat, and turned to Mr. Woddle.

"It looks as if we do have a little feathered friend on the loose, Mr. Woddle. Not quite a duck, but it seems you were on the right track."

Ted, Kai, and I hurried away in the opposite direction, trying not to break into fits of giggles.

"The attack of the killer mutant pigeon," laughed Ted. "Good one, Kat."

"Genius," Kai agreed.

When we opened the door, we found the space had been completely redecorated in rainbow colors and was covered in dragon footprints. Dodger was chewing happily on the ears of the box robot, which had been decorated with sweet wrappers and obviously still had the scent of something delicious on them. He had upset an easel with paint pots, and his scales were now speckled orange, lime green, and red, and his claws and tail were dripping paint.

But there was no sign of the other dragons. We searched the closet in a panic, but they weren't in the backpacks or hiding away in any of the boxes.

"I don't understand," Ted hissed, while Kai bundled Dodger back into his bag. "The door was shut the whole time; they couldn't have got out."

And then I saw the hole high up in the wall of the

closet. Where the grill covering an air vent was hanging loose.

"Look!" I pointed. "They must have got out through there."

Before I could climb up and peer through, we heard an earsplitting shriek, quickly followed by the sound of something metal clattering to the floor.

We hurried out into the corridor. There was another clatter and Liam came flying out of the double doors at the far end and ran right past us, clutching his backpack to his chest.

"What's up with him?" Kai hissed. "Not like him to miss an opportunity to get us into trouble."

"Yeah. What's his game? I bet he's up to something really evil," said Ted. "Lulling us into a false sense of security while he hatches his ultimate dastardly plan."

But we didn't have time to wonder about the inner workings of Liam's mind or what his evil plan might be, because just then, the double doors burst open again and Mrs. Battenberg, the cook, came charging through.

"Bat!" she howled as she sprinted past us. "There's a huge flapping bat in the cafeteria!"

"The dragons!" I hissed. We raced off down the corridor and as we skidded into the cafeteria, heapings of mashed potato hit us in the face. Sunny was

sitting in a tray of the stuff, his tail flicking great lumps of it into the air as he burrowed his way through the rest. Meanwhile, Crystal had successfully iced the entire kitchen counter and was happily devouring the chili. I looked around for Flicker, but couldn't see him anywhere.

Mrs. Battenberg's prize herbs in their little individual

plant pots, usually so neat and well cared for, were strewn across the floor. Soil and long, dangly roots were scattered everywhere.

Kat, who had come running in behind us, picked up one of the plants and tried to stuff it back into its pot. But it was way too big for the container in her hands. She looked between the plant and the pot, unsure what to do next. In the end, she shoved the plant into a saucepan and left it spilling out over the sides.

"What a mess!" she moaned.

An upside-down pan started edging its way across the floor towards me. I reached down and lifted it up. Flicker flew out and rose up to perch on my shoulder. I thought for a minute he'd turned a dark brown, until I saw the gravy dripping down my shirt.

"Not you, too," I said, shaking my head.

5
A Mound of Trouble

By the end of school that day, the story had taken on a life of its own. The imaginary unruly pigeon that had started the whole thing had been transformed into an irate ostrich. An ostrich that had escaped from a local farm and tried to trample Mrs. Fear in the corridor as it made its escape from Mr. Woddle. He, in turn, had been trying to lasso it with a fire hose. And Mrs. Battenberg's lone bat had become a whole colony of blood-seeking vampire bats that had threatened to attack the whole cafeteria. You know, we probably could have got away with telling the truth and no one would have batted an eyelid in our school. Even so, we didn't think we'd risk it.

One thing was clear: If we wanted to keep the dragons, we really needed to find a way to teach them some basic commands. You know, like: stop, stay, don't demolish the chili—that kind of thing. We spent the rest of that afternoon at Kat and Kai's trying to come up with ideas.

Because I'd been the one who'd first found the dragon fruit and Flicker, I think everyone expected me to know what to do. But honestly, I was as clueless as the rest of them. Flicker had always come to me and followed me of his own accord, not because I'd trained him to do it.

I was very aware that I was not fulfilling my role as Grand High Dragon Master. Which meant I needed to up my game and figure this out.

When you have a dragon, you have to expect the unexpected. So, when Kat and Kai's mom dropped me off at home that day, I wasn't as surprised as you might think to find what greeted me when I opened the door.

First off, there was my dad with his head in the downstairs toilet. Then my mom with two ferrets cradled in her arms and a cockatoo clinging to her hair. And finally my little sister, Lolli, shrieking with laughter and running in circles, dressed in a pair of gardening gloves and a tutu. A *very muddy* tutu.

"They're just here for a few nights so I can keep an eye on them," Mom said as the cockatoo launched itself from her head. "But I'm afraid these two might have had a disagreement with your robe. Sorry about that, love. Bit of a troublemaker, this one." And she stroked the silky fur of the snowy-white ferret who eyed me as beadily as Liam.

Being a vet, Mom often brought animals home "to keep an eye on." Sometimes they even stayed for

months, if they were strays and she had trouble finding them a home.

"It's OK, Mom," I said.

The truth was, the furry duo had done me a favor. It was Flicker who had destroyed my robe with his treading claws, and I'd been trying to keep them out of sight ever since. I would have pointed the finger at Tomtom—he was getting the blame for a fair bit of dragon damage—but lately, our cat had been keeping a very low profile. Probably wise under the circumstances.

"Thanks, love. Oh, by the way, don't use the toilet."

I turned and saw Dad, a plunger in his hand, ready to reach down into the stinky depths.

"At least not till Dad's finished fishing," Mom added.

As usual, Dad was plugged into his headphones with the music turned up so loud, you could have sung along to it halfway down the garden. He was nodding to the beat so manically, I was afraid he would actually lose his head down the toilet as well as the plunger.

"It's blocked," Mom went on. "Flooded everywhere." She made a face and I realized that, having kicked off my sneakers, my socks were now squelching on the carpet. I hastily jumped onto the first step of the stairs.

I thought of all the dragon poop I had flushed down the toilet in the last few weeks. As you know, dragon poop is explosive, but only if it dries out. So I'd figured the best thing to do was get to it quick and stick it down the toilet. That way, it couldn't detonate. But I always flushed, so surely it couldn't be that, could it? Then again, I had also hidden a few bits of dragon-destroyed evidence down there. You know the kind of thing: burned socks, chewed-up letters, the odd bit of scorched homework.

I gulped. I wasn't sure what I was going to do with the poop if it started blocking the drains.

Just then, Dad shouted, "Eureka!" and started waving a threadbare sock puppet in the air. Its googly eyes were spinning wildly and its wonky grin was even more wonky now. I breathed a sigh of relief. It was Lolli's. It looked as if I wasn't the only one hiding things down there.

I could feel Flicker starting to wriggle in my backpack, so before I could get roped into ferret-watching or toilet-plunging, I hurried away upstairs to my room. Except Lolli saw the backpack moving and immediately followed me, calling, "Mewannaflicka!" all the way up.

Lolli was the only other person in the family Flicker had allowed to see him. And she was besotted with the little dragon. And who could blame her, really? A real live, pocket-sized dragon living right there in your house!

Flicker was great with her, too. He flickered sparkly gold whenever he saw her. And he didn't even mind when she tried to feed him with her doll's fake milk bottle or bounced around my room with him stuffed into her sweatshirt like a mommy kangaroo. Sometimes I found him blowing warm breaths on her toes as she drifted off to sleep. And then she'd have an even bigger grin than usual on her always-sticky face.

"Mewannaflicka," she giggled as she came in after me.

"Just a second," I said, lifting Flicker out and setting him on my bed. "Give him a chance. He's been cooped up in there—he probably needs to fly."

Sure enough, Flicker soared up into the air and started whizzing back and forth. Lolli jumped around madly flapping her arms, trying to take off after him. She chased him, squealing with delight when he sent out little smoke rings for her to bat away.

I didn't want Mom hearing the noise. Lolli might be small, but she has the footfall of a baby rhino, so in an attempt to calm her down, I grabbed a book and waved it at her.

"Story, Lollibob Bobalob?" I said, using her full nickname to be sure to get her attention. "Your favorite."

She flapped over and flopped onto my lap, leaning back on me like I was a chair. Her thumb went into her mouth as Flicker in turn settled on her legs. By the end of the story, my butt was completely numb, but at least everyone was calm and I'd been in the house a whole half an hour with no mess to clean up. Which was definitely a plus.

Sadly, the lack of mess didn't last. When we headed down to find some snacks for us, and some broccoli for Flicker, Lolli took my hand and pulled me into the living room first. From the lack of parental shrieking, I could only think that the ferrets and the toilet had kept Mom and Dad too busy to notice what Lolli had done in there. Because what she had done was make a monumental mess.

I understood now why her tutu was quite so dirty.

In the middle of the carpet was a huge mound of mud. Wet, mucky footprints led in and out of the patio doors to the garden. Several upturned plant pots littered the floor and Lolli's pirate bucket and spade were lying on the sofa, leaving soil smeared across the cushions.

"What have you done, Lolli?" I hissed. Lolli and I have this unspoken pact that we stick together. And I owed her big-time for keeping Flicker secret and saving the day in Grandad's garden, back when cabbages were flying and Grim was about to launch another attack. But even I didn't know how I was going to talk us out of this one.

"Mewannadagon," she said with a smile.

My eyes fell on the mound. There was something sticking out of the top. I leaned forward and pulled it out. It was a pineapple. Now a very dirty pineapple. And suddenly, I knew exactly what Lolli had been trying to do. She must have decided a pineapple would be the next best thing to a dragon fruit. And she had planted it, hoping to grow a dragon tree of her own.

"Oh, Lolli," I said. "I think—"

But what I thought was cut short by the rather loud scream coming from my cockatoo-hatted mom.

6

Carroty Cowell and the Mud Monsters

By the time we'd cleared up the mess, we looked like a family of mud monsters. The bucket of water Lolli had helpfully poured over the pile of mud to make things clean again hadn't been a great success. Little rivers of mud streamed across the floor, spreading the mess even further. Dad had stepped in to take control, but actually stepped on Lolli's spade, slipped, and fell face-first into the muddy mound, splattering us all. Even the ferret wasn't looking quite so snowy.

When the doorbell rang, we all looked at each other, wondering who was in the best state to answer the door.

"If it's Mrs. Snoop from number ten, I'd rather no one answered it," said Mom. "She'll have a field day seeing the state of us. She already thinks I'm a bit odd after she came round and saw Eunice and Terence."

Eunice and Terence were the pythons Mom had looked after last year. I imagine most people would be a bit startled if you answered the door with those draped around your neck.

"You go, Tomas. You're a boy. She'll expect it from you."

I was going to protest—she was usually the last person to believe girls couldn't get just as messy as boys. And, after all, Lolli was twice as muddy as any of us, which just went to prove it. But I could see she'd reached the end of her usually quite long tether, so I let it go.

I squelched my way down the hall and peered through the mail slot. And grinned at the carrot waving to me from the other side.

"It's OK," I yelled to the waiting mud monsters. "It's just Grandad."

"Just Grandad, is it, Chipstick?" Grandad said as I opened the door to let him in. "Just Grandad? Well, there's a welcome for you, I must say. And there was I thinking you were my number-one grandson."

I was actually his only grandson.

I laughed and cleared my throat. "Ladies and gentlemen, your attention, please." I paused and did a drumroll on my leg. "It's the one . . . the only . . . the INCREDIBLE . . . Grandad."

"That's a bit better." He laughed. "Still needs some work, mind you."

He turned to brace himself for the hurtling mud missile that was Lolli.

"Bit young to worry about mudpacks, aren't you, littl'un?"

He lifted her up, not seeming to mind the mud she was getting all down his jacket.

"Megroodagon," she babbled.

He gave her a grin and winked at me.

"Well, that sounds just great."

Luckily for me—and Flicker—no one really bothered to listen to what Lolli actually said. They usually just smiled and nodded.

We all crowded round the kitchen table to see what Grandad had brought. Most days, he turned up with a fruit or veg box of some kind, and right now it was strawberry season. My favorite. I'd eaten so many of them one year, I'd broken out in a rash. No one had dared to explain why and I got to stay home from school, eating more strawberries to make me feel better. Best result ever!

As Grandad unloaded the berries, Lolli grabbed a handful and squished them into her mouth. Sweet, red juice mingled with the mud and dribbled down her chin.

He'd also brought the latest of his VIPs—Vegetable Impersonator Produce.

He held up the carrot I'd seen through the mail slot. It wasn't like the carrots you see in supermarkets. All neatly packed in a cellophane bag, all the same size, all the same shape. Grandad's carrots—and all his veg— were like us, covered in mud. And really strange shapes. This one had split in two at the bottom so it looked like it had legs. And the sprouts off the top grew like wild hair. It even had knobbly bits poking out the side as if it had its hands on its hips.

"Thought this one looked a bit like Ringo Starr."

I knew Ringo Starr was a musician in this band called the Beatles because Dad listened to them all the time and had old-fashioned records with with their faces on them. If you ask me, the carrot didn't actually look

like Ringo at all, but it was pretty fun writing out the name tag and lining it up alongside fellow carrot Simon Cowell, potato Paul McCartney, and string bean David Beckham.

"So, up for a bit of hard work?" Grandad asked me.

I nodded, my mouth too full of strawberries to answer properly.

The truth is, I owed Grandad a visit. Well, I owed him a lot more than a visit. Without his grand idea to clear the end of his garden, I'd never have found the dragon fruit tree or carried the dragon fruit home that first day. The same fruit that Flicker had burst out of in the middle of the night. I also owed him for looking after me so well when I was little and had a sickly heart, even though he always said you don't owe your family for that sort of thing; it's just what they do.

But I had promised to help him in the garden, and ever since Flicker and the other dragons had arrived, I really hadn't spent much time doing that. I popped in and out to keep an eye on the tree, but until there was a new crop of dragon fruit to keep an eye on, raking weeds and picking slugs off leaves couldn't really compete with spending time with a dragon.

"Don't worry about his dinner. I'll feed him," Grandad said to Mom as I raced upstairs to change my mud-splattered clothes.

"Fancy a trip to Grandad's garden?" I said to Flicker, whose claws were shredding one of my comics into pieces to line his bed in the toy box. There was no way I wanted to leave Flicker behind, especially not with beady-eyed ferrets patrolling the house. And he knew the way. He was used to following me, flying from tree to tree to keep out of sight. I opened the window for him and looked across the rooftops to the park and over towards Nana and Grandad's house beyond. I watched Flicker dart up into sky and then headed back downstairs.

As we turned into the park, Grandad stopped to rescue a snail slowly slithering its way across the path. Most people wouldn't have even noticed the tiny creature, and some like Liam probably would have made a detour to squish it if they had, but Grandad's philosophy was "Let all things be." It was part of the reason why gardening was proving a challenge. Lots of people would have chucked a load of weedkiller and pesticide over the garden. Grandad said the farmer behind their house did it all the time, spraying everything in sight. But Grandad was different. He was as organic as they came. Which is why I was stuck with a bucket for collecting slugs.

Flicker had stopped, too, and was peering down at Grandad from the branch above. I just hoped he didn't sneeze and rain sparks down on us.

"You off with the fairies again?" Grandad asked after he'd placed the snail on a nearby bush. He looked up to where I'd been gazing. Flicker thankfully had already flown to the next tree.

"Feels like I'm talking to myself half the time these days," he added.

I gave an apologetic smile. It was true. A large chunk of my brain was currently tied up reliving the chaos in the cafeteria. And the rest was in a spin trying to think up how to train the dragons and worrying about keeping them secret from nosy Liam. Any part that was left was keeping an eye on Flicker. How I didn't fall down through lack of available brain power was quite a miracle.

"So what's been going on with you and those friends of yours? You used to bend my ear no end with all your shenanigans. What's new?"

What's new, of course, was dragons. So all the stories I had to tell were about Flicker and Crystal, Dodger and Sunny. I racked my brain for something I could share with him. But there wasn't anything. I chewed my lip. And then shrugged.

"Nothing really."

"Busy with school. That it, hey? Them teachers keeping you busy?"

I nodded awkwardly. I hated fobbing him off with a fib. It was like when I hadn't told him about being in Grim's garden that time, or admitted that we'd all been out of the tent the night we had camped. I used to tell Grandad everything and I wished I could now. It suddenly felt like all the little thorny fibs were growing into a great big prickly bush between us.

When I didn't answer, Grandad gave a little sigh. His twinkly eyes closed for a second longer than usual as he paused to take a sniff of a rose in a hedge. He pulled it towards me so I could take a whiff.

"There's always time to stop and smell the roses," he said. "However busy and complicated life gets. Remember that, Chipstick."

7
A Grim Old Day

While Grandad rooted about in the shed for the tools, I inspected the dragon fruit tree. Its long, knobbly, cactus-like leaves sprouted out like unruly hair. I could see a few vivid yellow and orange tendrils starting to appear and knew that one night soon, the moon-white flowers would bloom. These amazing flowers, some as big as my head, appeared for just one night. Like starbursts they glowed, shining in secret through the darkness. Then the petals drooped and the first fruit of the next crop would start to grow. And there'd be more dragons to look out for!

The tree looked a bit more droopy than usual. I poured some water onto the base of it, soaking the roots like Grandad had shown me with the apple trees. It had been hot for weeks and he said everything needed a good, long drink. I also made a mental note to keep a closer eye on the tree from now on.

"Ho ho ho," Grandad said as he came out the shed waving a hoe at me. "Time to battle those weeds, Chipstick. Then we can spread that there mulch. It'll keep the water in and the weeds out." He pointed to

a huge heap of bark chips and my shoulders sagged at the thought of lugging all that across the garden.

Grandad must have noticed, because he put down his hoe and headed back into the shed.

"What do you say to a bit of fuel first?" he said, reappearing with a tin crammed with Nana's jelly doughnuts and chocolate fudge cupcakes. "I keep a secret stash down here," he chuckled. "Your Nana thinks old Mrs. Doodah's dog ate them."

I bet she didn't. Nana knew Grandad far too well. But it made us both laugh all the same.

While Grandad returned to the shed for a flask of coffee for himself and a bottle of lemonade for me, I threw a jelly doughnut into the air like a mini Frisbee. Flicker zipped down from the apple tree, caught it in midair and whisked it away.

I once heard my mom telling someone that gardening was good for you, that it kept you fit like doing a workout. I hadn't believed it. Wandering around pulling a few dead roses off a bush didn't seem like it would do much at all except bore the pants off you. But since coming to Grandad's, I could see what she meant. It was hard work. There was always some job to do. It was a shame I couldn't swap places with Flicker. After an energetic dust bath in the ashy remains of Grandad's bonfire, he was curling up to sleep in an old flowerpot. Lucky him!

After about an hour of hoeing, weeding, and watering, Grandad had me washing the plants. I know, weird or what? But it was one way of dealing with the pests without spraying them with chemicals.

It wasn't just slugs we were battling against. There were spider mites, aphids, blackfly, caterpillars, snails, beetles, wasps, earwigs, stink bugs, and more. It was a full-on assault. On our side were an army of ladybugs and lacewings that Grandad had bought online. They were the natural alternative to chemical sprays. But I felt as if we were in danger of losing the battle as the enemy marched on, chomping its way through our hard-worked-for fruit and veg.

Grandad wiped his forehead with a hanky and blew out his breath. And then suddenly, from across the fence, an even more beastly enemy loomed.

The huge shape rose up and peered over at us. Grim. His eyes were narrowed and the frown lines set so deep across his face, honestly, you could have skied down them. He also had what appeared to be a lump of jelly stuck in his hair. I looked up to see Flicker hiding among the leaves of a tree, nibbling on a piece of pastry. It looked as if the jelly doughnut filling hadn't made it up there with him.

"Hello there, Jim," Grandad said cheerily.

There was a grunt that was loaded with more grump than a bad-tempered camel who'd found you standing on his foot.

He glared at me. And swiped at a wasp that was now dive-bombing his head in an attempt to get to the jelly.

"Bloomin' bugs," he said. "They're all over my veg."

"Pesky little things, aren't they?" Grandad replied.

By the way Grim kept his eyes on me, I could tell he seemed to

be blaming us—or at least me—for the onslaught.

Grim's hand touched his hair and came away covered in sticky raspberry jelly. I stifled a smirk. He narrowed his eyes even more, staring at the soapy bucket I was still carrying as if it was full of jelly ready to lob at him.

"He'd better not be flinging bugs over onto my garden," he growled.

I had, in fact, done exactly that the first few times. Released the little band of renegades over the fence. To pay "Grim Jim" back for shouting at Grandad that time. But Grandad had caught me and that was the end of that.

"Or anything else for that matter," Grim added.

And he disappeared back to his shed, still muttering about pesky bugs and pesky kids and wiping his hand on his trousers, which only spread the sticky mess further.

I couldn't help myself and the smirk erupted into a guffaw. But Grandad's hard stare soon stopped it.

"Why's he got sheets covering his window and locks all over his shed?" I asked. "What's he got in there anyway?"

Grandad looked across towards Grim and the shed, then shrugged and handed me a rake.

"Nothing valuable, I don't expect. He just doesn't like nosy people. He's all right—just a tad grumpy, that's all."

"A tad?" I snorted.

"All right, a big tad. But just let him be, Tomas," Grandad said, digging his hoe into the hard ground. "He's still in a huff about old Mrs. Dollopsy-Whatsit, or whatever her name is, complaining about the smoke

68

from his bonfires. He's none too happy about having to cart everything away to the dump when he's always had a good bonfire to get rid of the garbage."

He gave a grunt as he bashed a clod of earth into bits.

"Besides, it's a busy time for old Jim. There's the annual County Flower and Veg Show coming up and I've heard he always does really well. People can get real competitive when it comes to the size of their onions. If growing the biggest veg was an Olympic sport, he'd be up getting gold, that's for sure. You should see the turnip he's got growing over there—he'll need the whole village to pull that out before long."

"So are you thinking of entering?"

"Maybe," Grandad said, scratching his whiskery cheek. "My beans are looking pretty prizewinning. Never seen ones so big."

"You should," I said. "Mom says you've always had green fingers. You're bound to beat the competition." I couldn't help enjoying the thought of Grandad outgrowing Grim.

Grandad laughed and I had a feeling he'd seen my eyes flicking over to Grim's shed when I said it.

"How about you and that sunflower, Chipstick? Going to beat the competition for the biggest and best?"

I grimaced and held up my fingers. "Not looking very green to me." The truth was I hadn't given much thought to the sunflower I was supposed to be growing for the competition at school. Compared to dragons, sunflowers didn't seem that exciting!

Grandad smiled and turned away. But as he headed off, he wobbled unsteadily, as if his foot had met a bit of uneven ground. He sat down heavily on the bench outside the shed.

"Time to close up shop, I think," he sighed. But he stayed there for a few minutes getting his breath back while I gathered things together and tidied up the tools.

I couldn't help peering over the fence again.

Grandad was right—the turnips and onions Grim was growing were huge. My eyes locked on the fortified shed where he was holed away. It seemed to me that Grim was way more than just a bit grumpy and I'd have been willing to bet that there was something going on in that shed that he really didn't want people to see.

By the time we'd had dinner—Nana's shepherd's pie followed by strawberry shortcake—Grandad had perked up again.

"Best be getting you back," he said.

"Take some pudding for Lolli." Nana smiled.

As we left the house, Grandad peered down the lane.

"Hey, isn't that one of your crew, Tomas?"

I looked to where he was pointing and saw Liam coming towards us.

"Er . . . no. Definitely not," I said.

"Well, he looks a bit like someone's pulled him through a hedge backwards. Perhaps you should see if he's all right."

I doubted Liam would like anyone fussing over him, least of all me. But Grandad was right about the

72

state of him. I could see now that his shirt was ripped on one side and he was limping. He looked up and saw us, then quickly turned on his heel and hobbled away.

What had Liam been doing down the lane? It only led out to the fields. And he was usually really fussy about looking well kept. So what exactly had he been up to?

8
A Flicker of Help

Back at home, I got ready for bed. Mom came in to say good night, bringing the beady-eyed ferrets with her. They squirmed in her arms, trying to jump loose, and I wondered if they could smell Flicker's smoky breath in the air. I'd have to make sure my door stayed firmly shut. Next came Dad, ready to "wrap and roll." His tuck-ins were legendary, leaving us "as snug as a bug in a rug," all cocooned in quilt. But tonight after he'd left, I wriggled out of my mummified state and sat at my desk, staring out of the window. Flicker flew over to join me. He laid his wing over my hand, then nudged my fingers so he could tuck his head under them. He peeked out and I smiled as I felt his comforting warmth on my hand.

But it didn't stop the mess of thoughts tangling themselves up in my head. Liam was up to something. I was sure of it. Which meant it was more important than ever that we had a way of training the dragons to make sure things didn't get too out of hand.

Out of the window, all I could see was fog. If I was in a book, I bet Miss Logan would say the weather was mirroring my head. Showing how unclear my thoughts were and how I was lost in a fog of confusion.

"What am I going to do, Flicker?" I whispered.

I stared out, willing the fog to clear inside my head as well as out there in the garden.

"We need something to help us. What is it that dragons love?"

Flicker started wriggling frantically. I looked down and he sent out a spray of sparks that shook me out of my daydream. He rubbed his head along the back of my hand. I smiled.

"It'd be easier if the others were like you. You're no bother. But they're all getting to be more of a handful. I just wish I could think of something. I feel like everyone's relying on me to come up with a brilliant idea."

Flicker nudged my hand, then launched up into the air. He circled above me, sending sparks raining down, then began zipping back and forth across the room. Something seemed to have got him riled up and I wondered if one of the ferrets had sneaked back in. But the door was still shut. Then he moved from sparks to blasting out fiery breaths that would have rivaled Sunny's. He dived down and incinerated the crumpled pieces of paper from my math homework.

"Hey, stop that," I hissed.

But he ignored me and simply grabbed another ball of paper in his claws. He swung it up and I watched it ignite under another fiery breath. This time he flicked his tail through the debris, scattering ash into the air. It drifted down onto me. I batted it away crossly and scooped up the remaining balls of paper, shoving them into a drawer out of his reach. But Flicker just set to work on one of my comics, shredding strips off it and blasting them to ash.

What on earth was he doing? Maybe I'd been wrong about Flicker being less trouble than the others after all!

"Enough already," I sighed.

He landed on my bookshelf and I scooped him up.

"Can we just go to sleep?" I said. "Maybe it'll be like Dad says and my brain will come up with the answer while I dream."

Flicker's scales shimmered bright red as I curled up in bed and tucked him in next to me. I really hoped Dad was right. I drifted off to sleep with Flicker's eyes twinkling up at me.

In my dream, I was flying. High up in the clouds through a purple sky. Green and turquoise light

swept in brilliant waves all around me. Below were mountains, rock, snow, and ice. I spotted waterfalls and crystal blue lagoons and cracks in the ground where fire boiled and bubbled below the surface. I swooped low, skimming over geysers with their jets of water bursting out and traced the curve of glaciers that creaked and sighed in their ancient voices. On and on I flew, until I saw the looming shape of a volcano. And I knew this was the place I had been seeking.

The air was full of ash. And when I reached it, I circled above the crater, faster and faster. In a dizzying dance.

I opened my eyes and flung off the covers as if the heat of the volcano was real. Next to me, Flicker was pulsing red and orange. A fiery glow in the darkness of my room.

9
The Fog Clears!

When I crawled into the Dragons' Den the next day, I found the others toasting a towering stack of pancakes.

"Brain food," said Ted, grinning and licking golden syrup off his fingers.

Kai tossed me one that Sunny had just turned a lovely golden brown.

"So, my best ideas definitely need syrup. How about you? Do you think better with syrup or chocolate sauce with sprinkles?"

"I think this might be a syrupy-chocolate-sprinkles-with-extra-whipped-cream kind of problem," I said.

"You've not had any luck either with the training then?" asked Kat.

I shook my head. "Sorry."

For a few minutes, we let the pancakes do their work, but no amount of syrup seemed to help. So I decided to fill them in on seeing Liam outside Grandad's.

"He looked a real mess," I said. "There's definitely something weird going on with him."

"Maybe it's something he ate," said Ted. "Mom won't let me eat blue sweets because she reckons they make me get all hyper."

"Maybe he's got a part-time job as a scarecrow," Kai suggested.

"Or he's doing a sponsored limp for charity," said Kat.

"Whatever's going on, you can bet it's going to mean trouble," I said.

Now that the pancakes and treats had been demolished, the dragons were getting fidgety. Crystal kept icing Dodger's claws to the branches he perched on and blasting icicles that rained down on him. He, in turn, was getting more reckless with fiery breaths to melt it all. It had always been a bit of a squash in the den, and more so since the dragons had arrived. But with ice and fire in there now, things were getting a bit hair-raising. I sighed as I stamped out another smouldering twig.

Suddenly Flicker circled the den, his scales shimmering yellow, orange, and scarlet. He landed on a branch at the back of the den and stared out across the field on the other side. He hopped from foot to foot and I realized he was going to take off. I reached out to grab him. But it was too late.

He flapped away over the field. Everyone crowded round, pulling back the branches to see more clearly.

"Where's he going?" Kai asked.

But I had no idea. He was all the way across the field already, almost at the lane that led to Grandad's house. He didn't look as if he was stopping. But then the next second, he dive-bombed the ground.

When he didn't rise up again, my heart stopped.

Had he just crashed? I tore back the branches and squeezed my way out of the den, scratching my arms and face. I didn't care though. Behind me I could hear the others wrestling their way through. But I was away already. I'm not the fastest runner in my class, but at that moment, it was like I was flying.

When I got to the other side of the field, Flicker wasn't lying in a crumpled heap on the ground. Thank goodness! He was flickering like a beacon, hopping up and down, scratching at the ground and sending clouds of dust into the air in the process. I ducked as I felt Sunny's wings brush the top of my head and watched as he, Crystal, and Dodger zoomed towards Flicker and what I now realized was the remains of a bonfire. One by one, they wriggled and rolled in the ash.

I thought of Flicker taking a dust bath in Grandad's garden and then burning things in my room. And of the dream, how it had felt like coming home as I flew over the volcano. And now this.

Flicker had been trying to tell me the answer all along!

As Ted, Kat, and Kai joined me, breathless and panting, I couldn't help grinning. Flicker flew over and landed on my shoulder, sprinkling me with ash.

"Yeah, yeah," I said, laughing. "I get it. Finally! Sorry for being so slow."

The others looked at me like I'd gone batty.

"Ash," I said, pointing to the ground and giving everyone a huge grin. "Dragons love ash."

Although we still didn't risk taking the dragons back into school, things got a whole lot easier after we found out about the power of ash. The dragons were drawn to it like Ted was to chocolate chips. We assigned clicks and whistles to commands instead of words. And the dragons were a lot quicker to learn than Dexter, Kat and Kai's terrier pup. They got the hang of picking things up and bringing them back to us in no time and after that, the games quickly became more advanced.

Kai started Super-Sticky, where he filled balloons with lemonade, then got Dodger to collect and drop them on command.

Flicker and I raised the bar after Flicker started making smoke rings and Dodger got the idea to swing the water balloons and release them through the smoky circles. Ten points for making it through the ring, twenty if it then hit its target underneath as well. The target usually being Ted.

"Leave off," he cried, as another balloon burst, soaking him yet again. "Anyone'd think I had a bullseye painted on my head."

"Now there's an idea," Kai laughed.

When the twins got tired of this target practice, they came up with an altogether deadlier game. Which they named Blast Attack.

Sprinkling a little ash on their wrists, the twins made a clicking sound somewhere at the back of their throats. Immediately, Crystal and Dodger zipped down from the branches where they had been perched, landed on the twins' arms, and dug their claws into their sleeves. Crystal lowered her head. Then she coiled her tail around Kat's forearm, her purple scales curling upwards along her sleeve. Dodger did the same on Kai.

The twins took a few steps away from each other, one arm held out in front of them, the other hand resting on their dragon.

"Ready?" Kat called.

"Born ready," Kai replied, his eyes locked on his sister's.

Kai lurched to one side as Kat's dragon let out an icy blast. Kai pointed his arm at his sister and returned

a fiery blast from Dodger. For the next few minutes, Ted and I watched an awesome battle of fire and ice, which the dragons appeared to be enjoying as much as the twins. They raised and lowered their heads and flicked the tips of their tails as they unleashed blast after blast.

It didn't take long for Ted to join in. Sunny soon got the hang of shooting flames at his opponents, although, having just eaten, his aim and reach was a bit more unpredictable. I was also slightly worried what might happen to Ted's arm if his dragon let out a

fiery fart rather than a belch.

I couldn't help being a bit envious. Blast Attack didn't seem to be Flicker's kind of thing. He didn't breathe fire as much as the others—or ice for that matter. I wasn't sure he'd be able to keep up. I watched the others roaring their battle cries as ice met fire and steam filled the air.

Suddenly, I felt Flicker's weight on my arm and winced a little as his claws gripped through my sweatshirt. His tail coiled up my arm and I smiled, feeling the heat of his little body.

A shiver ran along his spines and he pulled his wings back, lowered his head, and then unleashed a bright blue flame. It rocketed across the den, the tip of it spreading out in flickering white.

Flicker could breathe fire like the best of them! He also had the most accurate aim by far, and in between blasts, he puffed out smoke, which confused the others.

A true tactical warrior!

10
Slugs, Sunflowers, and Slime

"I wouldn't," Ted said the next morning as I flopped onto his bed.

My hand wavered in front of my mouth, the pancake I'd just picked up from his desk half in and half out.

"That one's Sunny's."

"You mean you're giving your dragon first dibs over your best friend?" I asked.

"It's not that," Ted said hastily. "I mean it's one of Sunny's specially prepared delicacies."

I looked at the pancake in my hand and the treacle dripping from it.

"Looks OK to me," I said.

"Sure, if you like slug slime on your morning treat."

The pancake shot out of my hand as I hurled it across the room. I screwed up my face.

"Sunny is a bit of a gourmet," Ted said. "The other day he brought me marmalade chocolate fingers. They were great. But sometimes his tastes can be a bit of a stretch—like these and the greenfly pancakes. He brings them like little offerings. So you have to be careful what you accept because you'll hurt his feelings if you spit it out."

I looked up at Sunny, who was watching me from the top of the closet. I shrugged apologetically and tentatively picked up the slime-smothered pancake, holding it out for him.

He swooped down and plucked it from my fingers.

"He's got quite a collection of slugs now," Ted went on. "I thought he was eating them, but he just seems to want their slime. Maybe it's like honey for dragons."

I gave a shudder and tried not to think about the slug farm developing up on the closet. I had visions of them in hamster wheels, their juice dripping into tiny thimble-sized buckets.

"So where's your sunflower?" I asked. "I left mine at home in the end. It's sort of . . . well . . . it's not what you might call thriving."

The truth was, the sunflower I'd been growing for the school competition had been sadly neglected. I'd eventually found it this morning under my bed. It hadn't even grown past the seedling stage. All it needed, Miss Logan had said, was some sun, some water, and a little care. Well, it hadn't got any of those since Flicker had arrived.

"Mine's struggling, too," Ted said.

And he pointed to a blackened plant pot and the shriveled remains of a sunflower head. "It got fire-belched."

Outside the school gates, we met up with Kat and Kai. Kai had a similar story with his sunflower. There had been an exploding poop incident on Dodger's first day, and the flower had never recovered. Kat however had somehow managed to keep her sunflower safe. And it was enormous. Taller than their dad, who was strolling up the playground with it, the huge yellow flower head nodding above him.

"It's brilliant!" I said. "You're bound to win with this, Kat."

She smiled and then leaped forward to stop her dad from face-smashing the closed door he was about to walk into.

Everyone had been looking after their sunflowers for weeks. And today we were supposed to be planting them along the school wall. At the end of the school year, whichever one had grown the tallest would win the prize. So far, Kat's was the biggest by a mile. Almost as big as the smile she couldn't stop from spreading across her face.

It would be great to beat Liam at something for once. He always had to be the best at stuff or have the best thing. Even in show-and-tell, he'd do the most extravagant yawn to make it clear that whatever was being shown couldn't impress him. But if I thought Kat's skyscraper of a sunflower was going to wipe the smug look off Liam's face, sadly I was wrong. Because just as we were settling down on the carpet, Liam swaggered in. At first I thought he'd messed up. He was empty-handed and I couldn't help hoping that, like me, he hadn't even managed to grow a seedling, let alone a flower.

But then I saw him looking past us out to the

playground. Twenty-five heads turned in unison. And then, twenty-one breaths were released in an awed "Whoa" and everyone hurried to the window to stare out. Only the four of us stayed silent, eyes fixed on the colossal towering stalk, its leaves like dinner plates and its huge yellow sunflower head as big as a beach ball.

"How?" Kat whimpered.

Liam sauntered up next to her, smugness oozing from him like slug slime onto a pancake. "Well, if you've got the know-how, you know how," he said. "Some of us just have it." He looked Kat up and down. "And some of us just don't."

Poor Kat's eyes filled up with tears and she pushed past him and hurried out of the classroom.

Ted and I glared at Liam, and then Kai, who probably should have known better given that Miss Logan was hovering behind, shoved Liam. He stumbled back and knocked into the table. The yell he gave when his leg banged it was louder than anyone

expected. Trust Liam to make it look ten times worse than it was.

"Kai, that's enough," Miss Logan said sharply.

Now you see why we call Liam, "King of Trouble." Although after what happened later that week we might have to change that to Emperor of Trouble.

11
Sneakier than a Ferret with a Meatball Sandwich

"Tomas, are you listening?"

It was dinnertime and as usual I hadn't really been listening to my mom at all. I was too busy thinking about Flicker and the other dragons. And watching Lolli finger-painting a face on her plate with meatball sauce. But in the end, it's hard to ignore someone who is waggling a forkful of spaghetti under your nose.

"Make sure none of your sillier classmates upset the animals on your school trip when you go," she said. "I'm relying on you to keep an eye on them. The Caldwells" donkey is a bit of a nervy old thing at the best of times.

And maybe you can keep an eye on that poor Liam Sawston. His mom's ever so worried about him."

Hang on, what? Poor Liam? Suddenly I was listening.

"I saw her at the pharmacist's earlier. He's got a nasty burn on his leg. He'd been messing about in their shed and she thinks he must have spilled something on himself."

I pictured Liam limping the other day and how he had yelled out after banging into the table at school.

"People can keep all sorts of toxic things these days," Mom went on. "Although she says her husband swears blind he doesn't use pesticides and all that stuff."

"Sounds just like Liam to be messing about with stuff he's not supposed to," I muttered crossly.

Mom looked at me.

"Oh dear, are you two not getting along anymore?" she asked. "That's a shame."

I nearly choked on my meatball.

"What do you mean, 'anymore'?" I spluttered. "We were never friends in the first place."

Mom smiled. "You and he were best buddies back in nursery school. The two of you were so sweet together. I'm sure he hasn't changed that much."

I stared at her.

"We were what?"

"Come on, surely you remember? You were inseparable when you went to the Happy Meadow Center. I guess when you went off to school and Ted was there, you just forgot all about Liam."

She reached out and caught one of the ferrets as it launched onto the table and started to make off with one of Lolli's meatballs. "All I can say is I'm glad Grandad's

got the sense to keep his garden organic. I wouldn't want to think of you messing about with chemicals."

And then the image of Liam's monstrous sunflower popped into my head. And it hit me.

Was that how Liam had grown such a huge flower? Had he really used chemicals?

He was as sneaky as that ferret licking his lips as he eyed up another meatball. He was such a cheat.

Mom was wrong. There was no way I had ever been friends with Liam. Just no way.

When I told the others about Liam and the chemicals, they were as angry as I'd been. I didn't tell them what Mom'd said about me and Liam being friends—that really would have horrified them.

"We need to keep an eye on him. Now we know how he plans to win the sunflower competition, maybe we can stop him," I said.

"At least he can't do anything with the sunflower today," Kat said. "Not with the school trip happening."

That was true, but if we thought giant sunflowers were our biggest problem, we were about to discover just how wrong we were.

The school trip to Caldwell Farm was meant to be the big finale of our Animals at Large topic. The farm was owned by Mrs. Caldwell and her grown-up son. She was a bit of a local legend, having won the great inter-village Frisbee-throwing championship twelve years running. People said her right arm was so powerful she could throw a disc clear across the English Channel on a good day with the wind behind her.

Her son was probably the tallest person I'd ever seen and had long, straw-like hair that drooped so far down over his eyes that you had to wonder about his ability to drive the huge red tractor he careered around on.

We hadn't taken the dragons back into school since the pigeon-bat-attack incident, but we figured they'd be no trouble on a farm trip, not out in the open. Besides, now we had the ash, we were feeling a lot more confident about things.

Miss Logan and Mr. Firth set off at a brisk stride while, like the animals marching onto the ark, we followed along behind in our pairs. Apart from Liam, who was swaggering along on his own and talking loudly, showing off to Amira and Jody in front of him about how he'd once spent a day as a VIP at a safari park and so basically knew everything now. The dragons, aware we had a hefty supply of snacks and ash in our backpacks, flitted back and forth above us, keeping to the trees.

When we got to the farm, we were welcomed by Mr. Caldwell. Or rather he stood there pointing down the dirt track that led into the farmyard. Mr. Firth started handing out clipboards and pencils and explaining what we were expected to do, and more importantly, what we were expected *not* to do.

"No upsetting the animals. No feeding the animals. No shouting near the animals. No climbing over fences. No eating anywhere except the lunch tables. No touching farm machinery. No . . ."

No one seemed to be listening very hard. We were all too busy taking in the sights. It wasn't your typical farm—that much was clear. Dad had said they were trying to "diversify," which basically meant they had to find new ways to make money since everyone bought their veg and milk from the local supermarket these days. He said the Caldwells had plans to revamp the farm and open it up to the public. The first thing they'd got was some more exotic animals, including, wait for it—crocodiles. Actual Nile crocodiles, which are like the most vicious crocodiles in the world. And as we looked across at the paddock, we saw an ostrich, a couple of llamas, deer, peacocks, and a donkey who looked about a hundred. There was also a play area with a fort made out of stacking crates and old wooden trestle tabletops laid over barrels, which I guessed was meant to be our picnic spot.

The place was awesome. And what's more, with clipboards in hand and dragons overhead, we were free to explore.

DO NOT FEED THE ANIMALS

12
More Trouble than a
Rocket-Propelled Bull

Thanks to Kai spotting the remains of an old bonfire tucked away behind a tumbledown shed, we found the perfect place to meet up with the dragons. They followed us there and we left them happily diving into the piles of ash while we headed straight for the crocodiles.

"Whoa, look at them," Ted said as we stared through the glass at the motionless creatures. "They're the armored tanks of the animal kingdom, the fiercest crocodiles of them all. You wouldn't stand a chance with one of them."

"Look, that one's got eggs," said Kat.

"Doesn't look very scary," said Liam, giving a fake yawn. "Bet it's stuffed. I haven't even seen it move yet."

Only Liam could fail to be impressed by a fifteen-foot-long prehistoric-looking crocodile. We watched him heading off until he disappeared behind the donkey's enclosure.

"Come on, let's look in those barns," said Kai, pulling Kat away.

The first barn we went into was home to a sow and her piglets, plus chickens, geese, and ducks who were free to wander as they pleased. There was also a really cool maze made out of hay bales that you could wander your way through, or, like Jack and Mahid, run along the top of.

But it was while we were playing in the maze that the first odd thing happened.

"There's a bull out there that blows smoke rings out its butt," Dylan said as he leaped onto the hay bale next to us.

"You what?" said Ted.

"Yeah, this mean-looking old bull in that field over there, it just raised its tail and we all thought it was going to do a poop but it actually blew this huge ring of smoke out. Weird, huh?"

Ted and I looked at each other.

We dashed outside in time to see a huddle of fascinated kids watching the bull intently. Thankfully,

whichever dragon had been sending out smoke appeared to have moved on.

"OK, we have a slight problem," said Kat, who had run over to meet us. "Crystal is trying to hatch one of those crocodile eggs!"

The little dragon had managed to get in through the skylight, and as we peered in through the window, we saw her perched on top of one of the eggs. The

mother crocodile was slowly coming out of the water, heading for the nest, her eyes fixed on Crystal.

"She'll eat her!" Kat cried. "Quick, do something."

But it was too late. The crocodile's mouth was opening wide, its jagged teeth poised, ready to snap down on poor Crystal.

"Look! It's eating its baby," Shanaya cried from behind us.

"No, no," soothed Miss Logan. "The mother protects the babies by carrying them around in her mouth. They're very good parents. Look, it says here that mother crocodiles look after their babies for up to two years. Most reptiles just lay an egg and leave."

"She thinks Crystal is her baby," Kat whispered with relief. "I do think we should still get her out of there though," she went on, "before that crocodile realizes her baby has wings."

We needn't have worried. Crystal obviously didn't appreciate being carried around in a cavernous toothy mouth. And, as the mother opened her jaws to lift up another egg, the little dragon shot out, skimmed across the water, and flew out through the open window. We followed her round to the back of the barn in time to see her let out an icy blast which froze the little duck pond in the field. But it wasn't over yet.

"Look—I think that ostrich thinks she's attacking her egg," Kat cried.

Crystal, having spotted the enormous ostrich egg at the mother's feet, had decided to have another go at hatching something. But the mother ostrich was not impressed. She plumped up her feathers and started chasing the dragon around the field.

Geese, chickens, ducks, and peacocks squawked and scattered as the huge bird flapped its wings wildly, running this way and that. Seeing an ostrich ice-skating across a frozen pond would have been enough for most of the class, but at this point, Dodger took up his place at the rear of the bull once more. This time he let out not only smoke rings, but a brilliant shot of flames.

"Told you," cried Dylan. "Rocket-propelled bull!"

The bull was understandably freaked out by the fire blasting from his rear end and started stampeding towards the gate. He only came to a stop just in time because a piglet landed on his head. Crystal had started collecting piglets and dropping the squealing creatures one by one into the paddock.

"I think it's time we rounded them up before this really gets out of hand," I said quickly. "You grab the piglets before they get trampled," I told Kat. "Me and Kai'll try to catch Dodger. Ted, keep your eyes peeled for Sunny and Flicker!"

I held out some ash. But the dragons were having way too much fun. And with a huge bonfire to play in, my feeble handful didn't hold much appeal.

Where was Flicker when I needed him?

"Found him," called Ted. And I looked across to where he was pointing.

It wasn't Flicker, but he had found Sunny. The dragon had discovered the picnic tables, which were now laden with Mrs. Caldwell's home-cooked scones, oddly shaped buns, and some wobbly-looking custard tarts. But it was the huge bowl of jam that started the food fight. Sunny had wriggled his way into the bowl and was flicking blobs of it out left and right. One of them landed with a splat on the side of Ella's face.

"Oh!" she shouted, as strike two hit her directly in the eye.

Assuming the jam had been a missile from Jack, who was stuffing his face with scones and tarts, Ella let off a return shot with a catapult improvised from a spoon. The lump of flying butter missed Jack but hit Stefan. Within seconds, half-eaten scones and tarts were whizzing across the table, covering everyone with jam and gloopy custard.

And then things really started to heat up. And by heat, I mean fire-sizzling hot. Flicker shot across in front of me and into one of the barns. I dashed after him. When I got inside, I nearly choked on the heady smell of blooming flowers. The place was a mess. Everything had been left to grow unchecked. Most of the plants were way too big for their little plastic pots, and others had latched onto the walls of the barn and were climbing up towards the roof, which had actually more holes than your typical roof. I spotted Flicker whizzing madly round between the stems of some huge blue flowers.

Suddenly the tickle in my nose got worse and I sneezed. Oh, no! If I was sneezing, then this was most definitely not the place for Flicker. But even as I thought it, I saw the little dragon hovering in midair.

"Flicker! No!" I yelled.

But it was too late. A ripple that started at his tail shuddered through him and a sneeze exploded out—and a fiery sneeze at that. I saw one of the blue flowers ignite and like a flaming domino fall towards its neighbor, spreading the fire in an instant.

But strangely, the fizzling flowers were not what had my attention. Because flapping out of the flames was a dragon.

And it wasn't Flicker.

13
Out of the Frying Pan, into the Fiery Inferno!

The dragon was bigger than Flicker—more like a fat pigeon. It had grey scales, a neat row of spines down its back, and a jagged, spiked tail that looked like a lightning bolt. It seemed to be having a whale of a time weaving in and out of the burning flowers. Every so often, it opened its mouth and let out a jet of green gas that made the air crackle.

The fire had spread even further now. It had already reached the plants that crept up the barn walls and was slithering its way up to the roof. The dragon seemed to be enjoying every new spurt of flame. It flew alongside it as though it were coaxing the flickering heat, urging it to grow bigger still.

Whenever a flower or a vine turned to ash, it did a loop the loop, sending out green sparks like tiny celebratory fireworks. I had a horrible feeling this dragon was not going to be satisfied till the whole place had gone up in flames.

I had to do something—but what?

I called out, but my voice was a whisper through the choking smoke. I flapped my arms, although what I expected that to do, I had no idea. Maybe if I could distract it, I could lead it outside. Or maybe Flicker would get the message and shepherd the new dragon out of the barn. But he was so small in comparison and I didn't like the idea of him getting in the way of one of those green blasts.

I was about to find out whether drawing attention to myself was a good idea or not, because the dragon turned. As it flew towards me, its scales and spines all suddenly stuck up and out, making it seem even bigger.

Underneath the grey, it shone a bright lime green. I couldn't help thinking it was like one of those puffer fish that blow up like a balloon when they're scared. I dived for cover as a green jet shot over the top of my head.

I watched as the dragon circled the barn, presumably readying itself for another attack. Now I knew how Ted had felt about being a target for the water balloons. All I could think was, where had it come from? There wasn't any more fruit on the tree yet. This dragon must have hatched in the last crop and not flown off with the others. But why?

Suddenly, Liam appeared at the barn door. I held my hand in front of my mouth, trying not to cough on the smoke and give myself away. I couldn't let him see what was in here. But while he stayed in the doorway, I was trapped inside a burning barn.

And then Liam did something that made me hold my breath even more. He lifted his hands to his mouth and blew. A hooting whistle a bit like an owl sounded through the air. And the lime and grey dragon suddenly stopped spewing flames and flapped down towards him. Liam scanned the barn and I saw his eyes finally fix on Flicker. He stood there for a moment, just watching. Then scowling, he opened his backpack and unceremoniously shoved the grey dragon inside. He muttered something under his breath and then turned and stalked out of the barn.

I don't know if it was the smoke or seeing Liam

with a dragon or realizing he had seen Flicker, but I staggered as I headed away from the cover of the hay bales where I'd been hiding. I lost my bearings and I couldn't see through the smoke to find the door.

I started to panic. And I felt my knees buckle. Then all of a sudden, a crackle of blue sparks lit up in front of my face, clearing the air just enough for me to see Flicker. He flitted down and gripped my sleeve with his claws. I reached out and touched him, focusing my thoughts on his little body rising and falling with every breath. Slowly, he pulled me forward. Coughing and spluttering, I let Flicker lead me out of the smoke and into the open. To my relief, it had started raining. A true downpour that was already putting out the flames. I stood there gasping in the fresh air, my mind still reeling from what I had just seen.

So now I knew Liam's secret. The problem was, he knew our secret, too.

14
Blabbermouths Can't Keep Dragons

"I can't believe it," Ted said, taking another huge bite of the candy apple he was holding.

"I can't believe you just fit that in your mouth," said Kat in disgust. And then added, "You're absolutely sure about this, Tomas?"

I gave them both a "you think I'd lie about something like this?" look.

"So he didn't get burned messing about with chemicals?" Kat said.

I shook my head. "Looks like he got on the wrong end of those green jets to me."

"It certainly explains all the weird behavior," Ted mumbled through sticky teeth. "I mean being too preoccupied to lay into us. And that fuss he made about his leg when Kai hardly touched him." Ted threw Sunny a lump of even stickier apple and the dragon's belly shone brightly as he gobbled it up.

"Trust Liam to muscle in on the best thing that's ever happened to us," moaned Kai.

"But when? And how? You think he really sneaked into your grandad's garden?" Kat asked.

I already knew he had.

"Don't you remember the night we camped?" I said. "After the dragons chased Grim away, we saw Liam in the lane. He must have followed us earlier, sneaked into the farmer's field, watched us catching the dragons through the hedge, and then waited till we'd left. He could easily have crawled through and caught one. There were still fruits on the tree. We were just too excited about catching ours to hang about."

Kai groaned.

"The question is, what are we going to do about it?" I asked.

"Whatever we do, it can't involve getting into any more trouble," Kat said. "Mom already erupted more spectacularly than that volcano Vesuvius when she found out about the farm trip."

I thought back to the lecture we had all had from Mr. Firth, and Mom's horror when she'd been informed of our part in it all. I guess I can see why he thought the four of us were entirely responsible for the utter devastation that our school trip turned into. As he'd come around the corner, he'd seen Ted covered in cake and pudding in the middle of the food fight. Then, beyond him, Kat with an armful of piglets, climbing over the fence of the paddock, and Kai chasing a hysterical ostrich. And then there was me, staggering out of the barn, leaving the nursery of flowers burning behind me. Whichever way you looked at it, it didn't look good. I'd just had time to see Liam smirking as Mr. Firth frog-marched us away.

"We are 'on very thin ice' apparently," Kat said, doing a surprisingly good imitation of her own mom.

"And it's not helped by those two," Kai said, pointing up at Crystal and Dodger. "It's not easy hiding two dragons."

"Especially those two," added Kat.

I watched Crystal frosting Dodger's tail. Every time he bashed the icicles away, she did it again. It looked like they were as good at winding each other up as Kat and Kai were. I guess they'd learned a few things from living with the twins.

"Have you noticed they're getting bigger, too?" Ted said. "Sunny used to be able to hide inside my jacket, but now I'd look as if I had a cushion stuffed up there."

He was right. Sunny had grown the most of all of them.

I glanced across at Flicker. I'd got used to him being small enough to tuck out of sight. I hadn't really stopped to compare him to the others. But as I looked at him, I realized he was now far smaller. In fact, I wasn't actually sure he'd grown at all. And I wondered again if, on that first night, I had knocked his fruit from the tree rather than waiting for it to fall like the others had—making him hatch too soon.

"You know, Sunny flew off with Ally's hamster the other day," Ted said. "Luckily I spotted him before the poor thing got taken out the window. I don't think he was planning on eating Hammy," he added defensively. "He was just showing him the sights."

I wasn't sure Ted's sister Ally would have believed

that anymore than we did.

"But we can't let Liam keep it," Kai said. "Imagine the trouble he'll cause, having a dragon."

I was also worried about how we were going to continue to keep the dragons a secret. I didn't want to think about what would happen if people got word of them. Images of cages and men in suits with clipboards prodding the dragons flashed into my mind.

"Liam's such a blabbermouth. I bet he won't be able to resist showing off what he's got," I said sadly.

"Well, we can't let it happen," Kai said. "We need to get that dragon back before Liam does anything stupid."

"Yeah, but how? I mean, Liam's not going to let us near it. And if he thinks we're after him, he could just tell everyone about us and our dragons."

For a while, we all sank into a pit of gloom. It sucked us down into its stinky murky depths; even Ted stopped reaching for food and his hand fell limply to his lap.

Eventually Kai stood up. He put his hands on his

hips, striking his best Superman pose. "Look, come on everyone," he said. "We need a plan."

Kat jumped up next to him. "Kai's right—we're always better with a plan. It worked for catching the dragons. We just need a new one."

"Sounds good to me," Ted said, his hand already reaching back into the candy bag.

I looked up at their faces. And then over to Flicker, who was staring out of the window. Maybe they were right. After all, we were the superhero squad. We could do anything.

15
Suspicions and Secrets

Operation Liam Watch got underway the next day. Kat had set up a schedule of our crew to keep tabs on him. Lolli and I were spending the weekend with Nana and Grandad so Mom and Dad could have a night away. It meant while I was off duty I could go and help Grandad and check on the dragon fruit tree.

The trouble was, things were still a bit awkward between me and Grandad. I got the feeling he knew something was going on with me that I wasn't telling him. Every so often over the last few weeks, I'd found him watching me, a thoughtful look on his face.

Thoughtful and a little hurt, if I'm honest. It wasn't going to be helped this time, with my head full of Liam and what he might be planning.

I found Grandad outside his shed talking to a jam jar. He gave me a nod and then tipped the jar to show me. It was full of ladybugs.

"Just talking to the troops," he said. "Right, you lot, look lively. Dotty, Scarlet, Midge, Mrs. Polka, I'm relying on you."

He winked at me and released the latest battalion of bugs into the garden.

"I'm hoping this lot'll sort out my beanstalks," he said. "I might have a handful of giant pods, but the plants themselves are looking none too happy. In fact, you'd best look lively too, Chipstick—that dragon fruit tree of yours is looking a bit sorry for itself as well."

Horrified, I raced over to the tree. Grandad was right. The droop had got even worse. Some of the tendrils had shrivelled up, and although there were one or two fruits, it didn't look like a great crop.

"What's happened to it?" I asked, my voice little more than a squeak.

"Might just be needing extra water, but these exotic types can be a bit temperamental," Grandad said.

A horrible feeling squirmed in my belly like a maggot wriggling through one of Grandad's pears. I'd tried to pay more attention to the tree after seeing how droopy it had been. But it was still struggling. What if somehow I'd done this? The tree had been fine until we'd cleared the garden—and until we had all started hatching our dragons. I'd always been so sure that Flicker's fruit had dropped into my hand that first day. And that the same had happened with the others. But what if I was wrong? What if we'd taken the fruit before they were truly ready and we had damaged the tree in the process?

The squeak of a wheelbarrow sounded from across the fence and I looked up to see Grim heading towards his shed. His barrow was full of boxes half covered by a tarp. When he saw me, he scowled, let go with one hand, and pulled the tarp all the way across, hiding the contents. I watched him wrestle the load across the uneven ground. When he finally reached the shed, he fumbled with the double padlock on the door.

I couldn't help wondering what was in those boxes. And more to the point, why he was being so secretive about whatever was in his shed? Maybe he was a bank robber and kept all his money in there, or a spy sending out secret messages in the dead of night.

I sidled along the fence, pretending to pick caterpillars off leaves but all the while keeping my attention fixed on Grim.

"Tomas," Grandad called. He shook his head and frowned. "You'll lose your nose in that there bush in a minute."

I stepped away, trying to act like I hadn't been spying.

"You haven't been over there messing about again, have you?" Grandad asked, giving me a hard stare.

"No way! What's Grim been saying now?" I said, launching into full-on defense mode.

"Now hold your horses. No one's been saying nought. And who's 'Grim' when he's at home?"

I looked sheepish and nodded over the fence.

Grandad sighed. I could tell he was going to do that thing where he stuck up for people, even people who totally didn't deserve it in my opinion.

"Just leave him alone, OK? He's had a hard time lately, poor Jim, so I've heard. He lost his wife a while back and his only son is off in Australia."

"But that's no reason to be having a go at us all the time, is it?" I snapped, even though I could feel another

134

maggot joining in the squirming in my tummy as I said it. I couldn't help feeling bad about his wife. But then again, I couldn't imagine Grim with a cozy home and a family. He was way too prickly for all that.

Grandad looked at me. His eyebrows wiggled higher up his forehead like two little fluffy grey caterpillars. I was still poised as if I was ready for battle right then and there.

"Just leave him alone. OK, Tomas?"

I mumbled something about it not being us who'd started it. And the caterpillars marched back downwards as Grandad gave me a warning stare.

As he turned to go into the shed, I saw Flicker dart past one of the tendrils on the dragon fruit tree and into the heart of it. He reappeared a minute later, but before I could peer in to look closer, Grandad called out again.

"Come on, Chipstick, let's take another look in that old book we found, see if we missed something about your tree."

Not wanting to draw attention to Flicker, who was now rapidly changing color, I hurried over to Grandad.

"Fancy crawling into a dirty corner?" he said with a little grin.

"What?" I said.

"I knocked the book off the counter earlier and it's fallen behind some boxes."

I followed him into the shed.

Grandad pointed under the counter that ran along one wall. "Just at the back there," he said.

I bent down and shuffled forward on my hands and knees, looking for the book. It was an old encyclopedia of plants that had been left behind by the woman who'd lived in the house before Nana and Grandad. I'd already been disappointed once by what I'd read in it. You see, it talked about this legend where dragons were supposed to breathe out the dragon fruit. But it didn't say anything about dragons actually hatching out of the fruit. Still, maybe Grandad was right about it helping us work out what was wrong with the tree.

It was definitely worth a look, even if it did mean scrabbling about on the floor.

"What is all this stuff under here?" I asked, dragging out box after box and trying not to think about the size of the spiders that had no doubt taken up residence in this neglected corner of the shed. They'd probably wear battle armor and ride mice.

"Dunno, most of it belonged to the lady who lived here before us. Elvi, I think her name was. The trouble is," Grandad went on, "when someone dies and they don't have family about to sort stuff, things get shoved in corners and forgotten. Nobody wants to spend time going through it all. We've stored what we can —photos and stuff. But I have to admit I haven't got round to looking through all this."

I reached in further and felt my way along. The tips of my fingers touched something. I felt the leathery spine and the embossed lettering and remembered how it had reminded me of some kind of ancient spell book.

I closed my eyes, ignored the mental images of

weight-lifting spiders, and stretched out till I could get my hands round it enough to pull it free.

As I lifted it, something that had obviously been tucked between the pages fell out. I picked it up and crawled out. Grandad took the book from me and laid it on the counter. He flicked through the pages till he found the one about the dragon fruit tree. His finger traced the words, hovering over certain passages.

"All it says here is be careful not to overwater it, so maybe it likes things dry, unlike the rest of the garden. I guess that makes a certain amount of sense, given it says it comes from Mexico originally. Perhaps we've been a bit too generous with the water sloshing?"

But I was only half listening. I was too intent on the piece of paper in my hand. I'd known the instant I saw it that this was something important. My fingers seemed to buzz just from touching it. Along the edge of the paper was curled a drawing of a dragon's tail. When I started to unfold it, I could see the whole shape of the creature, stretching out across the page. And within its wings was a map.

16
Dragons and Discoveries

"What you got there then, Chipstick?"

I quickly pocketed the map. And leaned over the counter, pretending to peer at the writing in the book.

"Oh, it's just something Ted gave me," I blustered. "Something he did for art."

I could feel the heat rising up in my face. My ears were positively sizzling. Grandad cleared his throat and I waited for his words, knowing full well he had seen enough to know it wasn't a kid's drawing. But they never came. He gave a sigh instead and reached over to fish some string out of a pot. As my eyes fell on it, I gave a little involuntary squeak.

"Is that yours, Grandad?"

Grandad, who was now winding the dishevelled string into a tight ball, looked back at the pot. "S'pose it is now—it's another leftover, like the book. Thought I'd keep my bits 'n' bobs in it. Pretty, huh?"

I nodded and when Grandad headed back outside, I pulled the pot closer. It was purple with flecks of gold, very pretty. But it was the tiny head peeking over the rim that I couldn't stop looking at. Stretching up the inside of it was a dragon, its tail swirling round and round the sides down to the bottom.

This had belonged to Elvi. Along with the book, and the map. Surely it all pointed to her having known about the dragon fruit tree in her garden? I thought again of its drooping leaves and shrivelled tendrils. If she'd known about it, maybe she'd left something that would tell us how to look after it properly.

The real question though—exploding and whizzing round my head like popping candy—was:

Had she, like Grandad, seen it as some exotic plant, or did she know more? Could she—like us—have known about the dragons?

One thing was for sure: I had to find out.

It was easy enough to persuade Grandad to let me cart the boxes up to the house.

"I could sort some of this stuff out for you, you know," I said. "Clear things up a bit in here. Make some space. See if there's anything worth holding on to."

Nana was less thrilled to see it all coming in. She looked up from the dining table where she and Lolli were making pastry shapes. Lolli had so much flour in her hair, it was white. She pointed to the shape she was squeezing with her chubby, and really quite grubby, fingers.

"Charlotte's making a dinosaur, I think," Nana said. "It's got great big spines and everything."

They weren't spines of course, they were wings. I could see that straightaway. Lolli frowned and poked a lump of pastry.

I bent down and whispered in her ear. "That dragon needs some fire."

She grinned and wiped a blob of jelly across the table to look like it was breathing flames.

Upstairs, of course, the first thing I wanted to do was to look at the map. I put down the last of Elvi's boxes, pulled out the map, and unfolded it while Flicker perched on my arm looking just as curious. A long winding river snaked its way up the paper with loads of little tributaries branching off. They stretched right out to the edges of the dragon's wings that framed the map. As I traced the widest part of the river, it was clear from the symbols that my finger was moving through thick rain forest. The only other features I could see were a few clear patches where the forest stopped. It was hard to imagine how anyone could usefully navigate it. I turned the map over, wondering if there was more detail on the other side. It was blank. Except, no, it wasn't exactly blank. There were the very faintest marks across the top of the sheet. I held it up to the light. But it was impossible to make out whether they were words or just the ink from the map soaking through.

I folded the paper and started looking through one of the boxes. It was full of masks and figures and animals made of stone and wood. I picked out odd-shaped bottles and little keepsakes like pan pipes and bangles. There were dog-eared travel books, too, and guides to far-off places: Indonesia, China, Bhutan, Mexico, Namibia, and Mongolia, and others. I flicked through a couple and found Elvi's name written inside. Elvi Jónsdóttir. Now that was a cool name!

Elvi must have spent a long time traveling and collecting stuff along the way. But there was nothing more about dragons or the dragon fruit tree that I could see in that box.

Lolli skipped into the room we shared when we stayed over and gave a little squeal when she saw the boxes, quickly followed by a frown. As if it was Christmas and I was opening presents without her.

"You can help if you like," I said. "I'm hunting for dragons."

Excited, she grinned and started pulling things out of another of the boxes, scattering them across her bed under the window. I looked at the mess she was making and wondered if maybe it hadn't been such a great idea to get her to help. Especially with all the dirt and dust she was unloading at the same time.

But after another few minutes, she lifted something out and made a little "oohing" noise. I glanced over and saw her holding a tin. It looked like a barrel-shaped cookie tin, except you wouldn't want to keep cookie in it because it must have been about a hundred years old and was pretty rusty.

"Dagondagon," she babbled.

And then I noticed the handle on the top was the arching back of a dragon. Lolli held the tin up to her ear and shook it gently. It made a quiet shushing noise, as if there was sand or something in it.

She held it out to me, jiggling it up and down. Flicker was changing color quickly, lighting up the air above us. He seemed just as excited as Lolli. I grinned and started to peel off the lid with my fingertips. When it finally came loose, we both peered in.

Poor Lolli's face crumpled. And then she sneezed as a smoky smell filled our noses. Inside was a heap of grey dirt. No, not dirt—ash. I think Lolli had actually believed she was going to find a dragon tucked up in there. Big fat tears started to roll down her face. Flicker flew down, for a moment his scales no longer bright. He wrapped his tail around her neck and sent a warm breath across her face that made the tears dry up. She sniffed noisily.

I found one of Grandad's caramels in my pocket. It was partly unwrapped and covered in fluff but it seemed to cheer her up. "Sorry, Lollibob," I whispered, "but this is still really important."

And it was. Because as well as the ash in the tin, there were marks on the inside. It looked like someone had been trying to work something out. First they'd written "Per day." Then "1 tsp," which had been crossed out, with "2 tsp" written underneath and also crossed out. The numbers kept on rising until they got to "5 tsp."

And the best thing was, I knew what it must mean.

We already knew that dragons loved ash. So what if dragon fruit trees loved it, too?

It seemed pretty clear that Elvi had been looking

after the tree, protecting it. And thanks to her, now we had some vital information to help us do the same. Maybe all I needed to do was to sprinkle ash on the tree and it would grow healthy again?

17
Things that Go
Bump in the Night

I was used to vivid dreams with Flicker curled up beside me. Imagining flying over strange lands of fire and ice, volcanoes erupting all around. They were happy dreams. But that night, my dreams were different. I don't know if it was finding the secret map or seeing all those travel books that did it.

I was high up, looking down on a forest that stretched on and on, as far as I could see. And there was a river twisting its way beneath me—and clearings. Just like on the map. Except in my dream, there were strange towers in the clearings. Buildings. Like a city.

And then I felt this intense heat. Flames were shooting out around me. I turned my head and saw wings. My wings. I was a dragon. And next to me was another dragon, soaring alongside, its eyes ablaze. We passed over the city, our great wings beating the air. Faces looked up at us. Hands were raised, pointing. Then suddenly, my stomach lurched and we dived down, down, down. Towards the canopy of trees.

As we got closer, we opened our mouths and fire burst from us, scorching the trees below. The land was burned. And we rose up, leaving nothing but ash behind us.

I woke up and flung the covers off, still feeling the heat of the fire on my skin. My heart was racing, whether through excitement or terror I couldn't tell.

Flicker wasn't curled up against me anymore but

perched on the windowsill. He was glowing fiercely, sweeping his little pointed tail back and forth.

Lolli was kneeling up on the bed and staring out of the window, her hands pressed against the glass.

"What is it, Lollibob?" I whispered.

She turned, rubbing her eyes and looking grumpy. Then pointed.

I knelt up beside her and peered out across the garden. At first, I couldn't see anything. There was just the inky night sky and the silhouettes of the crooked fruit trees.

But then right down the end, almost at the hedge, I saw a beam of light. It moved from side to side and then stopped. It was far too dark to see where it came from exactly, but I could guess. It must be Grim's shed. But what on earth was he doing out there in the middle of the night? What was so urgent it couldn't wait until morning or so secret it needed to be done under cover of darkness?

The next day, I couldn't wait to get out to the dragon fruit tree. While Grandad was still having breakfast, I took the tin of ash down to the garden. Easing the lid off, I started to scoop out five teaspoonfuls just like the instructions said. I sprinkled it over the soil, around the trunk, and then raked it in for good measure. The tree looked even worse than the day before; all the cactus

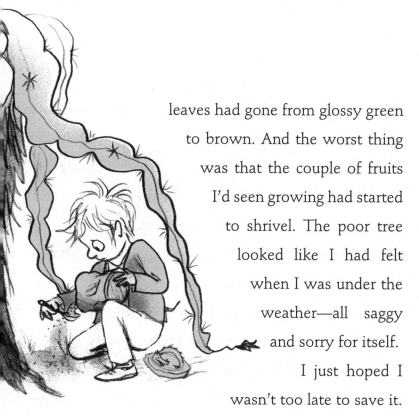

leaves had gone from glossy green to brown. And the worst thing was that the couple of fruits I'd seen growing had started to shrivel. The poor tree looked like I had felt when I was under the weather—all saggy and sorry for itself.

I just hoped I wasn't too late to save it.

The thought of the tree dying made me feel as if someone had used the spoon I was holding to hollow out my insides.

Later that afternoon, I met up with the others in our den.

"So do you think this woman, Elvi, knew about

the dragons?" Kat asked after I told them all about the map and the tin of ash.

I shrugged. "I haven't found anything to say she knew dragons actually hatch, but the map did have a dragon drawn on it and she was definitely looking after the tree. Maybe she was the one that planted it in the first place—who knows?"

"I kind of hope she did know," Kat said. "I mean, if your grandad's right and she didn't have any other family, it'd be nice to think that at least she had the dragons."

Her eyes fell on Crystal, who was frosting some cobwebs, leaving them sparkling in the sunlight.

I smiled. Although it was strange thinking of someone else knowing the secret, I couldn't help agreeing with Kat.

"Let's hope the ash does the trick and helps the tree," she said.

"So what's your news?" I asked. "What's Liam been up to?"

Kat delved into her bag and pulled out a chart.

She laid it in front of us, proudly. The twins had really gone to town on Liam Watch. The color coding alone must have taken them hours. But although it was undoubtedly pretty, I wasn't sure exactly how it showed Liam's movements over the past couple of days.

Ted leaned in, chewing the end of a felt-tip pen.

"So basically he's been in their shed apart from when he went to the park?" he said.

I stifled a laugh. Ted had a knack of getting to the heart of the matter.

"Well . . . yeah . . . basically," said Kai.

"And this black bit?"

"Er . . . that's when we followed him to the park but then we had to leave for our swimming lessons."

"And you were supposed to take over watching him," Kat added sternly, turning to Ted.

"Yeah, well, I've already told you about that," said Ted.

Ted had told us, at great length. He had been

having a few problems with Sunny. The dragon was eating and growing so rapidly it was getting harder for Ted to hide him and the damage he was causing.

"We think Liam must be keeping the dragon in their shed," Kai said.

"Poor thing," Kat said. "Locked up in there."

"Don't worry," Ted said reassuringly. "Now we know where he's hiding it, we can figure out a plan to set it free."

"Yeah. Simple," Kai said dubiously.

"It is," Ted said. "We just need a distraction."

18
Liam the Invincible

Kai was right to be dubious. Every morning we passed Liam's house and took a peek, hoping we might find a way to sneak in unseen. But Liam's mom worked from home, so even when Liam had football after school, we couldn't get near the place.

Luckily though, a few days later, I got my chance when Mom asked me for "a really big favor." The ferrets had been partying in the kitchen cupboards and thanks to the mess—and trying to find the sneaky pair—she was late to pick Lolli up from a playdate.

"Could you go and get her, love? I wouldn't

normally ask, but Finnegan is still hiding somewhere and I daren't just leave. It's only round the corner. She's at Bea's house."

Any other time I would have moaned, groaned, and downright refused this request. Not because I minded fetching Lolli, but because of where she was. The one house I'd usually go out of my way to avoid. But not today. You see, Bea was Liam's little sister.

This was a brilliant chance to get a closer look at the shed. When I got to the house, instead of knocking on the front door, I headed for the side gate. If anyone asked what I was doing, I could just say I was going round to the back door.

When I popped my head round the wall and scanned the garden, I saw Bea and Lolli playing in a big turtle-shaped sandbox. They had built a castle and were now decorating it with stones and sticks. A doll with no hair was propped up against one wall and Bea was holding a little pony, cantering it up to the drawbridge. Meanwhile, Lolli waggled a shark along the moat they had dug, making chomping noises as it chased the pony.

Suddenly Liam came out of the shed. He laughed when he saw the girls" castle and I thought for a second he was about to kick it to pieces. But then I realized he didn't need to. Because he opened his jacket and the grey dragon flew out. It flapped round and round above Bea's head. She sat there open-mouthed, while Lolli waved the shark at Liam and gave him her hardest stare.

What was Liam thinking? Anyone

could be watching from the house. But of course he was too busy showing off to care.

"What this fairy tale needs is a dragon," he said nastily. The dragon swooped lower and let out a blast of green. Bea twisted out of the way and fell backwards, landing on the castle and squashing it flat.

Both girls immediately burst into tears. I raced over and glared at Liam, who was so surprised to see me materializing in his garden that he nearly fell in the sandbox, too.

"What are you doing here?" he spluttered.

"Keeping an eye on you, that's what!" I snapped. "And just as well, by the looks of it. Why do you always have to cause trouble?"

Liam scowled. "Listen up, ant boy," he said, getting to his feet so he could properly tower over me. "I can do what I like." He brushed the sand off his pants before squaring up to me. "In fact, I can do whatever I like. Whenever I like. Wherever I like. And there's nothing you can do about it."

I felt myself bristling. "Oh, yeah? You'd better watch out, we're onto you. Whatever it is you're planning."

"You think so, do you?" Liam snorted. "It doesn't matter what I'm planning. I can do anything I want now. You can't tell on me ever again."

He leaned in close till I could smell his peanut butter and jelly breath and said, "Because I know your secret."

Then he looked up at the sky as if searching for something. And I suddenly felt very glad I'd left Flicker at home.

Liam lowered his voice, going for the full-on evil baddie hiss. "And I can tell everyone anytime I want. So you're the ones who'd better watch out."

Walking home with Lolli, I couldn't help thinking how complicated life was since the arrival of the dragons. It was all getting rather difficult, what with making sure the dragons stayed out of sight, clearing up unexploded poop, hiding any claw marks and burn marks, oh, and in my case, keeping an eye on two sneaky ferrets.

Then there was the very real worry of whether the dragon fruit tree would even survive. And now there was Liam and whatever he might be planning and how we were going to distract him long enough to rescue his dragon. And of course, whether we could do it at all without him giving the whole secret away.

That's an awful lot to think about, I can tell you. Just something to bear in mind, if you're someone who likes things simple. Because having a dragon isn't all playing games and toasting marshmallows—there really is more to it than that!

To deal with one of those worries—the state of the dragon fruit tree—I made sure that every day I got over to Grandad's to sprinkle the five spoonfuls of ash on it. I was tempted to chuck a whole load on at once, but I kept to the instructions Elvi had left. The last thing I wanted to do was make it worse. It was bad enough knowing I hadn't managed to look after it properly— what if it actually died under my care?

I thought it was making a difference. The leaves seemed to be getting greener and less limp, and even the shrivelled fruits looked as if they might be coming around. But it was hard to tell—it still didn't look very healthy.

But then Ted told me something that made me realize we were going to need more than ash to save the tree.

"Well, Dad's been asked to take photos of the County Flower and Veg Show, you know, for the paper. And while we were out, he got talking to one of the old guys who was entering. And he said he didn't know why he was bothering really because he never won anything. Everything he tried to grow just shrivelled up. And it was always the same old story of this one guy winning. And here's the interesting bit," and Ted leaned in ready to whisper, "he reckons this guy is using sprays and all that sort of stuff, which is completely illegal in these competitions. And he even said he wondered if someone hadn't been tampering with his plants. And guess who he was talking about?"

Ted gave me a meaningful stare. But I already knew.

"Grim!" I said.

It had to be. Suddenly it all made sense. Hadn't he been the one moaning about pesky bugs? Then there were those boxes he was hiding, his fortified shed and, most incriminating of all, the way he'd been creeping about in the middle of the night.

"Grim's cheating!"

"More than that," Ted said. "He's sabotaging the competition to make sure he can't lose."

The nerve of it! After all his accusations and wagging fingers, accusing us of doing things we shouldn't.

What's more, with his garden so close to Grandad's, the state of the tree made sense, too. He was killing it with chemicals. Whether he actually meant to damage the tree or not, it didn't matter. He was using them. It wasn't my fault after all. It was Grim's.

No wonder the ash hadn't been working! The poor tree didn't stand a chance.

"We need to get a closer look at what's in Grim's shed," I said. "We need proof."

Because I wasn't about to let anything happen to the tree. It was up to me to protect it. And I intended to do just that.

19
Revenge of the Scary Squash

Just when we thought we'd never get close to Liam's dragon, his shed went and blew up!

Or that's what it looked like had happened as we peered over the hedge on our way to school. Planks of wood littered the garden and flower beds. A giant—and I mean giant—beanstalk had burst through the shed, smashing the walls and lifting the roof clean off.

Now, I know what you're thinking—this is weird. Have we jumped into some kind of fairy tale? Are you telling me Jack's going to leap out with his fist full of magic beans and we're all going to hear a mighty voice like thunder rumbling, "Fee fi fo fum," and all that stuff?

Well, no. This isn't some fairy tale and we weren't immediately thinking we were going to be gobbled up by a giant. But sometimes real life can be stranger than stories. We knew that from the bizarre facts Ted regularly told us.

"That thing is humongous," said Kai, looking up at the beanstalk.

"I know. Those beans are as big as my arm!" I replied.

"What is going on?" Kat said. "First colossal sunflowers, and now beanstalks."

"I've heard of bamboo growing a foot in a day, but this is ridiculous," said Ted. He looked thoughtful. "There's a redwood tree in America called Hyperion which is three hundred eighty feet tall. Maybe it's a bamboo-bean-redwood hybrid."

"What it is, is weird," said Kai.

"Watch out," Kat yelled. "Incoming pod."

And we all scattered as huge beans started raining from the sky and thumping onto the ground around us.

"One thing's for sure—Liam is going to have to find somewhere new to hide his dragon," Kat called.

"Which means we need to keep a very close eye on him," I replied. "A very close eye indeed."

Since the art closet episode, we hadn't dared take the dragons back into school, but now things were different. We didn't want to be separated. Crystal and Flicker were small enough to hide in our backpacks, and Ted and Kai decided Sunny and Dodger should stay in the trees that lined the playground. We knew by now they wouldn't go far from the rest of us. Dodger was a master of staying out of sight. I just hoped Sunny wouldn't smell Mrs. Battenberg's school dinners and go looking for a snack again.

When Liam appeared in the coatroom, we all watched him like hawks. He scowled at us and threw his bag into a corner.

"Well, at least we know he's not keeping it in there," Kai whispered.

"He'd better not be, after doing that," said Kat fiercely.

Miss Logan appeared in the doorway and ushered us in. All morning, Liam kept looking out the window, or rather trying to look out. It was a bit difficult these days with his enormous sunflower blocking most of our view.

Even so, we all managed to see Mr. Peters, the pre-K teacher. He was coming down to the playground from the school vegetable garden, followed by his class and struggling under the weight of a monstrous squash. It was so big, he could hardly see where he was going. Until it exploded and then he could see just fine. Standing there splattered in mushy bits of vegetable, he got quite a cheer. He even took a bow—but then that's the kind of teacher he is. Liam was the only one not focused on Mr. Peters; he was staring off away from the playground.

"Something weird's going on around here," Kai said. "And I bet I know who's at the bottom of it all."

At lunchtime, rather than running off to play football, Liam loitered near Mrs. Olive, the midday supervisor. Every time he thought no one was looking, he peered through the gate of the school vegetable garden.

"You know, Liam's taking a very keen interest in gardening all of a sudden," Kat hissed.

"We need to get in there before he does and have a look around," I said.

Our chance came at PE. While the rest of the class jogged down to the far end of the field, we hung back and then ducked into the vegetable garden.

You know when you were little and you wondered what it would be like to shrink really small? To be like Tom Thumb or Mrs. Pepperpot or *Alice in Wonderland* when she's tiny? Well, when we swung open the gate, we knew how it felt. Because we were surrounded by giant-sized super-veg. The tomatoes were as big as our heads, the beans as long as our arms, and you could have made a hammock out of the rhubarb leaves. Mr. Peters hadn't even chosen the biggest squash, because Ted was able to climb onto that and sit on it like he was riding a horse.

"Good grief, look at this place!" Kat exclaimed, while Ted galloped his way to victory in a race against a giant turnip.

And then we saw the grey shape emerging from behind some Bunyanesque big broccoli. Liam's dragon had grown even more since I'd last seen it and, as we stood there, it let out a green jet at a row of lettuces. Incredulous, we watched the frilly green leaves stretching until they had more than doubled in size.

We all looked at each other, mouths gaping.

"Well, at least now we know for sure who's behind Liam's super-sunflower and Mr. Peter's exploding squash," Kai said. "And that giant beanstalk!"

"And remember Mrs. Battenberg's herbs in the school cafeteria? No wonder you couldn't get them back in their pots, Kat!" said Ted.

"Imagine getting served one of those vegetables," Kai said. "I have enough trouble with a few carrots."

"Your Lolli would think those really were trees if she saw that broccoli," Kat laughed.

"Well, whatever that dragon is doing to them, our tree could do with a bit of it. Shame it can't make that grow," I said sadly. "It was looking even worse this morning."

Kat held up the withered remains of one of the bean plants. "I don't know about that. Doesn't look like this super-sizing is doing much for the plants."

"Watch your heads," Kai said. And we all ducked as another green jet shot over us. The dragon flapped past us and settled on a bucket of compost. It eyed us warily.

"Come on, now's our chance," said Ted. "Let's grab it."

"Slowly," Kat said, reaching out to hold Ted back.

"We don't want to scare it."

But Ted had already lunged out. Alarmed, the dragon puffed up, its scales and spines sticking out, the lime now showing beneath the grey. It flapped up into the air and another green jet shot out. This one was coming straight for Ted. He dived behind the enormous squash just as the jet hit it. We watched as the squash grew . . . and grew . . . and then burst spectacularly.

The dragon disappeared over the hedge into the park beyond and we all scrambled towards Ted. He was scraping squash mush from his hair, his face screwed up in disgust.

"This stuff reeks," he moaned.

I grinned, relieved that it was only the squash that had been turned to mush.

"So now we know where it is," Kai said, "how are we planning on catching it?"

It was a good question. It didn't look like this dragon was going to come quietly.

20
The Hedge that Hung On

After school, we all followed Liam, keeping far back so he didn't spot us. He wasn't going his usual way home; instead he'd turned into the park and was scurrying along the outer fence where he was hidden by the trees.

"Where's he heading?" Kai hissed.

There was nothing but fields down this side of the park, unless he was going all the way across, to the lane where Nana and Grandad lived. I suddenly pictured Grandad's gargantuan beans and Grim's humongous onions. And my stomach did a monumental backflip.

"Oh, no!" I cried. "He's been in Grandad's garden. That's why all the vegetables have grown huge—that dragon's been breathing on them."

"What?" said Ted. "Why?"

And then a truly terrible thought hit me.

"What if Liam's been sneaking in to try and steal another dragon fruit?"

Before Ted could answer that, Kat grabbed my arm.

"I think he's calling it," Kat said. "Look, he keeps blowing on his hands."

Sure enough, the next second the lime and grey dragon darted down from one of the trees. Liam pulled off his coat and, as it flew in reach, he cast it over the dragon like a net. It dropped to the ground under its weight.

I heard Kat let out a little grunt of displeasure and mutter something under her breath about some people having no respect. Liam wrapped his arms around the bundle and lifted it up. It wriggled and squirmed.

"Come on, this is our chance," I said.

"Hey! Liam!" Ted shouted.

Personally, I'd been thinking of being a bit less obvious. You know, element of surprise and all that. But Ted's yell had shattered that. Liam spun round, saw us creeping up on him, and immediately started running. We chased after him, yelling at him to stop. But, of course, he didn't listen.

For a minute, I thought we had him. We were that close. But then he ducked through a gap in the hedge and disappeared. We scrambled after him, crawling on hands and knees through the undergrowth.

"Hey, get your butt off my face!" Kat snapped at Kai after a few minutes. "Get your face off my butt," he answered. "I can't go any further, so just stop pushing!"

I could see Liam through the tangle of branches, somewhere on the other side. He hadn't run off. He was just standing there.

"I don't understand," I said. "How did he get out of here? We've been crawling for ages and there's no sign of any exit."

And then I noticed the creaking. The branches around us were moving, and a sprig of leaves burst out right in my face.

"It's his dragon," Kat cried. "He's using it to make the hedge grow."

Suddenly I had visions of us all trapped inside the hedge forever, woven into the foliage. Looking around, I realized I couldn't see where we'd crawled in.

"We've got to get out of here," I yelled, spitting out a mouthful of leaves. Everyone started bashing

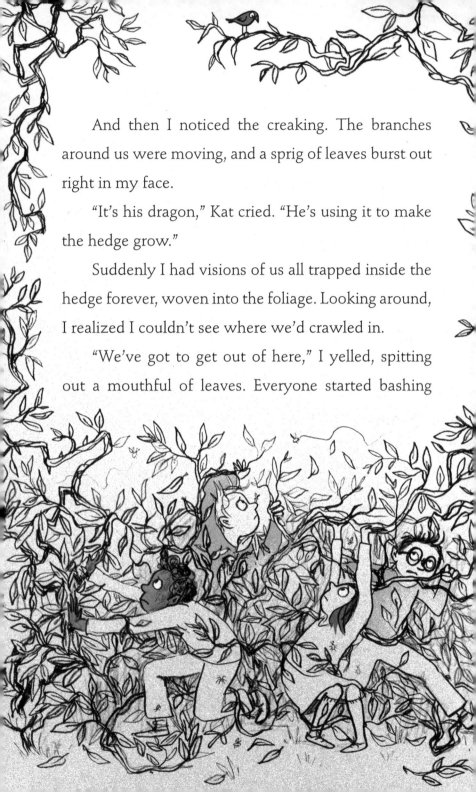

at the hedge. I think we were all starting to feel a bit panicky, knotted up in there. Our arms and legs were being scratched by twigs and we were covered in little bugs and beetles that seemed to be seeking safety in our hair.

"Fancy that—a talking hedge," jeered Liam. "Next thing you know there'll be magic dragons all over the place." He snorted with laughter and ran off, yelling, "Smell ya later, Whiffy Liffy."

I groaned. I knew I'd never live down that episode with the dragon poop in the dressing rooms. I'd have shouted something back, only I was afraid I'd swallow one of the wayward beetles if I opened my mouth.

So there we were, trapped in a hedge, and Liam was free to saunter away. And get himself to Grandad's garden, too. After all, what had he said about magic dragons all over the place? It was beginning to look like he really did have plans to get himself another dragon fruit.

I glimpsed Flicker through the prickly leaves. I called out to him and he darted down towards us. Motioning for the others to stay low, I gave him a nod and he unleashed a fiery breath at the hedge. Sunny and Dodger soon joined in and between them, they burned a gap wide enough for us to crawl through. Looking back at the sizzling leaves, I was afraid the whole hedge would go up like an inferno. But luckily Crystal froze the burning branches and stopped the fire in its tracks.

We stood there, nursing our scratches and picking the wildlife out of our hair and clothes.

Then we raced over to Nana and Grandad's house. But there was no sign of Liam.

While I hung around to help Grandad pick Nana a bunch of vegetables, the others trooped off home. I looked over the fence at Grim's enormous turnip and imagined Liam sneaking his way across to the dragon fruit tree. I couldn't believe he'd be stupid enough to try to hatch another dragon when he had his hands so completely full with his one. But then that was Liam for you.

There was something even more worrying to think about, too. And that something was the dragon fruit tree. Because it was looking worse than ever. It was pretty clear to us now that it was Liam's dragon breathing on everything that was making Grim's

vegetables so enormous. But Grim no doubt thought it was all the chemicals he was using. With such good results, he must have been chucking more and more onto his garden. Filling the soil with chemicals that were slowly but steadily killing the poor dragon fruit tree.

21
When Things Are Not What They Seem

So that's how we found ourselves back camping in Grandad's garden on Friday night. The day after we nearly got eaten by the hedge of doom, we'd all decided it was the best way to catch Grim in the act. And stop him before it was too late.

As I waited for the others to arrive, Grandad asked if he could have a "quiet word."

"Listen, Chipstick. Jim's been having some trouble again. Things have been damaged, and he's found footprints tramping all over his plot."

I hadn't been over onto Grim's side of the garden

since the night we'd gone looking for the dragons, but I still felt the color rising in my cheeks. It was like I was getting so used to feeling guilty about keeping secrets from Grandad I immediately went bright red.

"You're not messing about in there, are you? It's just that he's pointing the finger at your lot again."

"I haven't, Grandad. We haven't. We . . . I . . ." I shook my head. The truth was I knew exactly whose footprints they would be. The words were there, jiggling around on the tip of my tongue. I could just tell him right now. And he looked desperate to hear it. But I couldn't just blurt it out.

"Is there anything I should know, Chipstick? You know you can tell me anything."

I shuffled awkwardly from foot to foot.

"Apart from that rocky road is the best flavor ice cream—because we all know it's cherry vanilla," he said with a wink. I tried to ignore the twinkle in his eye that made him look forever hopeful.

Before I had a chance to mutter any kind of response, the superhero squad skidded up to us on their bikes. I never thought I'd need to be saved from Grandad, but relief flooded through me at the distraction.

"All right," I said to Ted, Kat, and Kai, who were looking from me to Grandad and probably hoping he wouldn't ask them anything either.

"All right," Ted said.

"All right," echoed Kat, and Kai.

"Talkative bunch, aren't you?" said Grandad.

We all laughed nervously.

"Remembered your tent this time then?" Grandad said, pointing to the bundle strapped to Ted's back. "Well, you know where everything is."

He waited a moment longer, looking like he was on the verge of saying something else.

"See you in the morning, I expect," he said at last.

I was pretty sure that wasn't what he'd been about to say. But he headed inside.

I told them about Grim having found footprints in his garden.

"Looks like you were right about Liam," said Ted. "That sneak!"

"Well, we can keep one eye out for him at the same time we're keeping the other eye on Grim."

Everyone nodded, and Kai went cross-eyed to prove it could be done.

We'd already sneaked out once while camping in Nana and Grandad's garden. Doing it a second time didn't feel any better. Especially after Nana made us all her special-occasion triple chocolate chunk cookies, some iced mini donuts and gave us a bag of Grandad's special toffee.

But we had to protect the tree. And if that meant sneaking back into Grim's garden to prove he was using chemicals to cheat at the show, and killing the tree in the process—then we had no choice. And if we found that sneak Liam at the same time, so much the better.

This time we pitched the tent down among the

apple trees. We'd be able to hear if Grim was up to anything and be close enough to catch him at it.

While we waited for it to get dark, we tucked into Nana's goodies and Kat and Kai told us how Crystal and Dodger had found my cat, Tomtom, creeping up on a baby bird and turned the tables by pouncing on him and then lifting him up in the air.

Ted laughed. "Fancy kidnapping Tomtom."

"Catnapping more like," Kat giggled.

I laughed, too. "I wondered why he'd been keeping such a low profile lately. I thought it was because of those ferrets Mom's looking after."

As time ticked by, we all started to yawn. One by one, we took turns to lie with our head out of the tent, keeping watch for any signs of Grim.

"I see something," hissed Kai, just as the rest of us were dozing off. "There's a light flickering over there at the bottom of his garden."

We all crawled forward to have a look, rubbing the sleep from our eyes.

"Right, let's get out of here," I said. "It's time to catch that sneaky cheat red-handed."

I winced and rubbed the back of my neck. Flicker's tail had scratched me. I lifted him off my shoulder. "I thought you'd got the hang of that tail," I said. "Keep to the trees. I don't want him seeing you." Flicker flew away from me and flared bright orange. He sent out a spray of sparks that crackled in the night air.

"What's got into him?" Kat asked.

"I don't know, but it'll have to wait. Come on."

We crept out of the tent and edged our way down the garden.

I hoped the dragons would keep to the trees and out of sight. But, following Flicker, they all flew back and forth down the garden. Then one after another, they kept flitting down to the dragon fruit tree and zooming away again.

"Maybe they know it's in trouble," Kat whispered.

Seeing the dragons in such a frenzy made me even more determined.

"Come on," I said, every inch of me prickling with the anticipation of catching Grim.

The light we'd seen had gone out, and Grim's garden and shed were in darkness.

As we approached, I realized I could hear a low murmur.

"Is that music?" Ted whispered.

I nodded. "It's coming from Grim's shed. I'm going in for a closer look."

As quietly as we could, we clambered over the wire fence separating the gardens and tiptoed towards the shed. Apart from the music, I couldn't hear any movement.

"I don't think Grim's in there," I whispered.

"What about the light we saw?" Ted asked.

"Maybe it was in the field—the farmer or something."

I peered around the shed door, which was open. A drifting, beautiful sound lifted into the air. It was coming from an old computer.

As soon as the dragons heard the music, they stopped their frenzied flying. They seemed to be drawn to the haunting sound and began to rise up. The four of them were circling slowly, weaving and twisting, following each other in a spiraling dance.

We watched, spellbound, as the dragons soared up into the sky, mesmerized by the swirling sound of the violins and cellos filling the air.

"Well, they obviously like it," Kat said, smiling.

"Why's he playing music?" Kai asked. "He's not even here."

Kat stepped into the shed and shone her flashlight around as the rest of us followed her.

"I think I know," she said. "Look at these."

The glow of the light fell on a magazine that was lying open. Kat lifted it up. There was an article with a picture of a man cradling a tomato plant. He had

a microphone in his hand and it looked like he was singing into it. The title said "Plants Love Music."

"It says here that singing and playing music to your plants helps them grow bigger and better."

Ted snorted with laughter.

"Yeah, I reckon it depends on your singing," said Kai. "The noises Kat makes would make most plants shrivel up." Kat shoved him and he stumbled back into a box of books.

The books had titles like *How to Grow Organic Vegetables*, *A Guide to Gardening the Natural Way* and *Bee Green*.

The music faded to silence. Kat looked at me and I started getting that uncomfortable feeling in the pit of my stomach again.

"Hang on—if he's all about growing things organically, why's he using chemicals?" Kai said.

"I don't think he is," Kat replied. She looked directly at me. "We just kind of assumed that, didn't we?"

"But then what's killing the tree?" I said. "Why

isn't the ash working? There must be some reason it's suddenly shriveling up." If I could have changed color like Flicker, I'd have been flaring bright orange, just like he did when Tomtom chased him and he was in panic mode. "It can't just be my fault," I said.

I heard the last words squeak out of me and realized just how responsible I'd been feeling for the state of the tree. After all, it had been fine before I found it.

Kat squeezed my arm and Kai shuffled closer.

Ted said, "It's not just you, Tomas. We're in this together, remember?"

Suddenly a light flickered through the shed window. We all ducked down, Kat fumbling with the switch on her flashlight.

"Grim!" she hissed.

"I don't think it is," I whispered. "It's coming from near the hedge, not the house."

We looked at each other through the gloom, all thinking the same thing. It had to be Liam.

Keeping low, we peered around the door. The

flickering light could be seen moving across the end of Grim's garden and into Grandad's.

"Well, that'll be the footprints Grim's been blaming us for," Kai said.

We waited for the light to stop moving. We knew Liam was heading for the tree. As silently as possible, we crept out and picked our way between Grim's vegetables. The ones closest to the fence were looking abnormally large, just like the ones in the school garden. It was pretty clear that Liam's dragon had breathed on them too at some point. Grim must have been over the moon to see the size of those onions!

As we got closer, we saw Liam bending down by the dragon fruit tree. He was carefully pulling the cactus leaves to one side, wincing from the sharp thorns. There had only been a couple of fruits on the tree earlier, and they were shrivelled up. So what on earth was he doing?

And then we saw him put his hands to his mouth and make that owl sound. From behind us swooped the grey shape of his dragon, flying so low over our heads we could see the lime green glowing under its wings. It settled next to Liam, and as he pulled the last cactus leaf aside, I saw what was hidden deep within the tree. Standing back, Liam clicked his fingers and the dragon let out a green jet that lit up the whole dragon fruit tree with an eerie light. He clicked his fingers again and the dragon breathed once more. And then again.

I remembered Flicker lighting up like a beacon that day with Grandad, and how the dragons had zoomed down to the tree earlier. They must have known what Liam was doing, what was hiding within the leaves.

And what was going on with the tree. We just hadn't listened. And I wished we had.

Because there deep inside the tree, so heavy that it was making the trunk of the poor tree bend under its weight, was a dragon fruit. Not a normal dragon fruit, one the size of a mango. A vast, giant-sized dragon fruit—as big as a football.

22
Super-Sized Trouble

Anger rose up in me and I stormed over the wire fence.

"Get away from that tree," I shouted at Liam, who was still crouching beside it.

Surprised, he wobbled on his heels and toppled over on the muddy ground.

"Ow," he yelled and pulled out a thistle the size of his arm from under his butt.

"Serves you right," said Kai behind me.

"Whatever you're doing, stop it!" Kat shouted. "You're killing the tree!"

"Baloney!" Liam said, scrabbling to his feet and looking round for his dragon. "I'm making things grow huge. Well, that thing is anyway."

"That THING?" shrieked Kat.

Liam really had done it now.

"You mean the awesome dragon you've been lucky enough to be looking after? Although looking after is hardly what I'd call what you've been doing. Besides," she added, "that dragon might be super-sizing the fruit and veg, but the plants are dying afterwards. It's draining all the goodness and life out of the soil and the plant. What's the use of one gigantic fruit if the tree dies?"

Liam looked round at the garden and shrugged like he didn't give a hoot about a bunch of stupid plants.

Kat launched herself at him, and for once I was the one holding *her* back.

"Listen, Liam . . ." I said. I took a deep breath and thought about Grandad.

Maybe I could employ a bit of his philosophy

about seeing the good in everyone and appeal to Liam's better side. I stepped in closer, keeping my voice as calm as possible. "The thing is, Liam, your dragon is causing chaos. And the more chaos it causes, the more likely it is someone's going to notice. We have to protect the dragons. And that means keeping them secret."

I waited, willing him to understand and to do the right thing. We all waited. Even the dragons seemed to stop flitting about above our heads.

But then he just narrowed his eyes and glared at us, taking his time to eye up each one of the superhero squad as we stood there together.

"You wait till I get a super-size dragon. Then you'll see some proper chaos." And he snorted out a maniacal laugh, reached forward, and grabbed at the fruit, which had now swollen to the size of a beach ball.

Wrapping his arms around it, he heaved. But it was far too heavy for him to move. He obviously hadn't thought this bit through. I almost wanted to laugh with relief. Except now the dragon fruit was pulsing a vivid green. The spiky skin started to ripple and I remembered the night Flicker had burst out of his fruit.

"It looks like it's going to erupt out of there," Kai said.

I nodded. "Get back, everyone!"

Liam stayed where he was, his eyes fixed on the fruit as it continued to swell. A grin spread across his face.

"This dragon's going to be epic!" he shouted. "It'll wipe the floor with your feeble, squirt-sized dragons."

He was acting like some kind of evil super-villain. I half expected him to rub his hands together, cackling gleefully.

And I guess he might have done just that, had the fruit not burst at that point and splattered him with huge quantities of green, foul-smelling goo.

"Slimed!" cried Kai and Ted in unison and high-fived, looking utterly delighted as Liam staggered around covered in smelly gunk.

Meanwhile the dragon that had hatched from the fruit had passed in an arc over our heads. As we watched, it landed pretty far away. It was the size of a large turkey and was a fluorescent green, which made it look almost radioactive. It raised its head, unfurled its wings, and shook its body. It shuddered and we all stared in horror.

"It's getting bigger!" Kat cried.

The dragon was indeed growing. It had gone from turkey to large cow in a matter of seconds. And it didn't look as if it was about to stop. With every shudder it expanded further, though its belly was inflating faster than the rest of it so its wings and tail now looked stubby in comparison.

Like Flicker when he was born, the dragon didn't seem to have control over its tail, which flung about wildly, ripping through Grandad's green beans and sending his sweet peas flying. Its wings obviously weren't up to getting it airborne, so it began to undulate its way across the garden, flattening everything in its wake.

When it had reached the size of a large, very fat walrus, it let out a rumble. A rumble that grew louder and louder until finally it opened its mouth and a green fiery belch exploded out of it. We all clasped our hands over our mouths and noses as the sickly green fog of belch breath drifted over us.

"That stinks worse than Dexter after he ate that jar of chilli sauce," Kai groaned.

"I thought Sunny was bad," Ted said. "That's a whole other level of rankness."

Liam, who was closest, stumbled around gagging, his face screwed up in disgust. His skin had taken on a green tinge of its own.

"I bet it's like skunk spray; he'll reek of it for days." Kat grinned.

Liam wasn't impressed. "It looks like a huge spiny winged slug," he whined.

"Oh, dear. Not living up to your expectations?" Kat said sarcastically. "What a shame."

He scowled at her and made a face. Then he picked up a strawberry that had been super-sized and was looking nicely fit to burst and lobbed it at her. It missed its target and splatted on the ground, but in reaching for another mushy missile, Liam slipped, staggered backwards, and actually bumped into the huge dragon's

rear end. Its tail swung up in the air and something truly noxious exploded out. If we thought the green gases from the front end were bad, they were nothing compared to this. It exploded out with such force that Liam was sent flying one way and the dragon actually lifted slightly off the ground and flew forward in the other.

"That's jet propulsion in action, that is," sniggered Ted.

The dragon seemed poised to capitalize on its first self-propelled flight of less than two feet. It had its eyes on Grim's super-size eggplants and a flimsy wire fence wasn't going to get in its way.

"We've got to stop it," I cried.

But how could we? It was getting bigger by the second. And so were its fiery belches. One of the trunks of the apple trees had already been left blackened.

We tried to form a wall in front of it. But you try facing down a ravenous, fire-burping dragon which is clumsier than you'd be after spinning upside down on a merry-go-round all afternoon. And there was no way any of us were going near its back end.

"What are we going to do?" Kat yelled.

They were all looking at me like I had some great plan tucked up my sleeve. I resisted shrugging helplessly and instead looked for Flicker, trying to buy myself a few seconds to think.

But a few seconds is all it takes for things to go from bad to very, very bad indeed. With another shudder, the dragon gained elephant stature. And its next belch set Grim's garbage cans on fire.

And then Kat squealed. And we all turned to see a tall figure striding down the garden through the darkness towards us.

23
Sometimes
It's the Little Things

The thing about a dragon the size of an elephant is you can't really hide it in your jacket. Or even stand in front of it whistling nonchalantly and hoping the person doesn't notice. And let's face it, when toxic-smelling green flames are lighting up the sky around you, there really isn't anything left you can do. So there wasn't much point trying to hide the truth from Grandad any longer.

He came to a stop in front of me, breathless and dishevelled. His mouth hung open and his eyes ping-ponged between me and the rather large dragon behind me.

Funnily enough, the main thing I felt was relief. It was as if the great big prickly hedge of fibs had been burned to the ground by dragon fire. I stepped forward and Flicker flew down and settled on my shoulder. His scales shimmered, flickering through every color.

For a moment, the chaos in the garden and the fire-belching dragon still setting things alight all went into freeze-frame. And there was just me and Grandad again.

I smiled. I couldn't help it. And the best thing—the thing I suddenly realized when Grandad's eyes lit up with that twinkle of his—was that I hadn't ever needed to grow the prickly hedge in the first place.

"Well, Chipstick, looks as if we might have something to talk about after all."

And he grinned.

There wasn't time for the whole story of course, but that could wait. He could see the problem. I had intended to point the finger at Liam, but the sneak was already legging it down towards the hedge, cradling the grey dragon who was still super-sizing things with every breath. Typical. Trust Liam not to stick around to face up to the trouble he'd caused.

"He'll have to wait," Ted said, watching Liam disappear. "For now, anyway. So what's the plan?"

Everyone was looking at me again. I looked to Grandad, but he shrugged.

"You're the expert, Chipstick. I'll follow orders on this one. Beans are more my area of expertise. All I've got is a raspberry net, and somehow I don't think that'll be much use for catching this fella."

I stared at the dragon who was chomping its way through some giant lettuces and demolishing the rest of Grim's vegetables with every flick of its tail.

"We need to get it up in the air," I said. "The dragons usually feed up and then fly off. That's what the others all did."

"Except for these guys?" Grandad said, looking up at Crystal, Dodger, Sunny, and Flicker, who were hovering above our heads.

"Well, yeah, except for them." I grinned.

"The thing is, those wings don't look like they'll get it very far," said Kai.

"You'd be surprised," said Grandad. "Think about bees. They don't look like they should fly, but there they go, buzzing merrily around. Maybe it just needs a bit of lift to get it going."

Ted looked at me. "Reckon a full-on fiery fart should do the trick. Let's help it by gathering up as much food as we can. If it's like Sunny, the more it eats, the bigger the reaction."

"Broccoli and beans!" Grandad cried. "That'll get it going. Well, it always works for me, anyway," he chortled.

We hurried about collecting as many vegetables as we could, and the dragon played its part by eating whatever we produced. Our own dragons joined in, dropping little offerings into the pile. Suddenly the dragon paused and its belly started glowing an intense lurid green. It shuddered and knowing what was coming, we all dived for cover.

Even the dragon seemed to know this was the one that would do the trick. It lifted its head and stretched up its neck, unfurled its wings, and readied itself for launch.

"Five . . . four . . . three . . . two . . ." called Ted. But before he got to one, the dragon blasted off. Choking on the smell from the green fog it had unleashed, we watched, hoping to see it soar skywards and away. But having got off the ground, the dragon just flapped around awkwardly a couple of feet in the air, sending out more belches that set light to what was left of Grim's vegetables.

"It's not going anywhere!" Kai cried.

"I can see that!" I yelled back. I called to Flicker. "We need your help, Flicker."

I stretched out my arm, looking hopefully at the little dragon. Flicker shone a brilliant red and zipped down towards me.

I grinned. "Blaster dragons at the ready," I called. Everyone soon figured out my plan and a moment later, we were all standing there with our dragons gripping our sleeves.

"We need to shepherd it upwards," I said desperately. "Stop it thinking it can hang around for another serving of lunch."

Kat lowered her head to Crystal and whispered something. Her dragon let out a shot of ice straight at the dragon's tail, making it twist away from the tree it was about to crash into. Sunny soon joined in, belching flames for all he was worth, and Kai and Dodger showed how the hours of water-balloon practice had paid off by launching cucumbers at the dragon whenever it started veering the wrong way.

The trouble was, with Crystal spraying out tiny icicles and Sunny's unpredictable flames, the lumbering dragon just seemed to get confused and blundered around even more. The final straw came when Dodger blended into the green of the dragon's scales, then suddenly darted out in front of it in a flash of shocking pink. The dragon was so startled, it started swooping down towards us until I thought it was going to crash-land.

Suddenly Flicker let go of my arm and I watched him disappear into Grim's shed. I couldn't blame him for getting out the way. I knew he didn't have the fire-power of Sunny or Crystal or even the stealth factor of Dodger.

Then I noticed Kat peering into the shed. She suddenly turned and called to me.

"Tomas, I think Flicker's got an idea."

I raced over and she pointed at him. He was hopping from foot to foot on Grim's old computer, his nose stabbing at the keys.

"The music!" I said, suddenly understanding.

Kat nodded. "They loved it, didn't they? Maybe if we play it, that dragon will calm down a bit."

"It's worth a try," I said. Flicker flitted out of the door as Kat bent over the keyboard.

"There's something called 'Pomp and Circumstance,'" she said. "What do you think dragons like?"

"I really don't think it matters," I said.

But I was wrong about that.

Kat's fingers tapped the keyboard and music blared out. It didn't sound very calming. Sure enough, when we dashed outside to look, the dragons were responding to the marching rhythm. Dodger and Crystal started hurtling back and forth over our heads and the huge dragon began thrashing and bucking madly.

"This is no good," I shouted. "It's whipping them up into even more of a frenzy. Try something else."

I watched Kat scanning the screen. "'Serenade for Strings,'" she cried. "That sounds more like it."

A brief silence was followed by an altogether calmer sound. Flicker started circling upwards, turning and twisting in a spiraling dance along with the lilting melody. We watched with held breath, waiting to see what the enormous dragon would do.

For a second, it didn't look as if the change of music

had had any effect, but then the huge lumbering shape stopped thrashing about and turned to look up. Its eyes locked on Flicker. The little dragon was spinning above its massive head, flickering different colors, blazing red and fiery orange and electric blue. He lit up the sky, shining brilliantly like a beacon.

Slowly, lifted by the music, Flicker rose higher. And the bigger dragon began to follow, captivated by the sound and mesmerized by the color-changing glow from Flicker's little form.

Then Crystal, Sunny, and Dodger flew in and joined Flicker in the dance, leading the dragon higher still.

"I think it's working," Ted shouted.

And we cheered them on, Grandad calling his encouragement along with the rest of us. Higher and higher the dragons flew. Until eventually the huge shape became a small dot and one by one, our dragons flew back down, returning to Ted, Kat, and Kai.

But I couldn't see Flicker. Grandad came and stood

next to me and rested his hand on my shoulder. He gave it a little squeeze. I wasn't worried. I knew Flicker wouldn't just leave. But I don't think I really let out my breath until I saw the little flickering orange glow appear again and begin to make its way down towards me.

Flicker settled on my shoulder. He curled his tail around my neck until the tip of it tickled my ear and nestled his head under my chin. As usual, his shimmering red body glowed like a hot ember. And right then as the warmth pulsed through me, I really felt as if I was glowing, too.

24
Deal or No Deal

I turned to Grandad.

"Grim's not going to be happy when he sees all this," I said. "You know, I thought he was hurting the dragon fruit tree. Turns out he was bathing his plants in music, not chemicals. He's as green as you are."

The truth was that after all that time thinking it was my fault, if I'm honest, it had been a relief to blame Grim. I'd been so busy pointing the finger at him, I hadn't seen what'd really been going on.

Grandad chuckled. "So, old Jim's not so bad after all then, huh?"

I raised an eyebrow. I wasn't sure I'd go that far, but I was sorry about the state of his garden.

"It's a terrible mess," I said sadly. "I'm not sure he'll be winning the annual show this year—not unless he's going for the smoothie category."

Grandad surveyed the destruction.

"Reckon you're right. And I don't think we'll be able to blame this on the pesky bugs," he said with a grin. He ruffled my hair. "We'll just have to tell him the truth."

I stared at him.

"We can't do that!" I cried.

"Hold your horses, Chipstick. Let me finish. We'll tell him the truth that there was an explosive gas incident in his garden. If he wants to think it's the methane in those compost bins rather than a massive dragon with stomach problems, then who are we to correct him, right?"

I laughed. "You really think he'll believe that?"

"I think most people would sooner accept that

than believe in dragons. Sad though that is."

"Sad for them," I said. "Not sad for us. We have to protect the dragons. We need to keep them secret. It's bad enough that Liam knows."

Grandad nodded and rubbed his chin, looking thoughtful. He didn't speak for a bit while he bent and picked up a snail slowly making its way over one of the enormous eggplants.

"It's good that you want to protect the dragons, Tomas. But you know you can't keep them here. Not really. You do know that, don't you?"

"What do you mean?" I said.

"Well, you saw what a mess that dragon made of everything."

"But that was because it grew so fast," I said quickly. "Liam's dragon breathed on the fruit and super-sized it. Ours aren't like that."

Grandad sighed. "Not right now they're not. But they will grow. And who knows how fast. You can't have four huge dragons living with you. Apart from anything else, I think people would start to notice them then."

I realized I was shaking my head. Inside, I felt my heart drop, squashing my earlier happiness like a brick flattening an overexcited cheerleading ant.

"I'm sorry, Tomas."

"But it'll be summertime soon. We've got so much planned," I pleaded.

Grandad smiled. "I bet you do. And we'll have a fair bit more to talk about now, won't we?" He smiled. "I've missed our chats."

"Me, too," I said.

"How about this: You keep them till the end of the school break. . . ." Grandad said.

My brain started spinning. It would give us some time at least. And maybe Grandad would change his mind.

"But then you have to let them go," he said, looking me straight in the eye. "Deal?"

I looked over to Flicker, perched on the dragon fruit tree. It was starting to look healthier already without the huge dragon fruit sapping its strength. Flicker shone gold and bobbed his head up and down, sending a spray of sparks into the air. With every atom of my being fighting this, I whispered:

"Deal."

I turned back to the others. Kat was cradling Crystal, who was breathing frost circles along her arm. Dodger had obviously decided there was no need to be shy around Grandad and had turned an electric blue. He was happily collecting raspberries in his claws and dropping them into Sunny's open mouth from ever greater heights.

"Now that's true friendship." Ted laughed. "How come I don't get to sit around while you guys feed me?"

"Here you go," Kai laughed, and threw a mushy raspberry at him.

"If I'd had time to actually open my mouth, that might have gone in," Ted said, wiping the splattered mess off his face.

I watched them lobbing raspberries at each other and wondered how on earth I was going to tell them what I'd just agreed to.

I thought of all the cool things the dragons could do. Crystal with her ice-breathing, Sunny with his awesome flames, and Dodger the ultimate in stealth. And then I thought of Flicker. Thanks to him, the super-size catastrophe of a super-sized dragon on the loose in our little village had been averted.

How could we ever let them go? And go where? We didn't even know where home was for the dragons.

But then I felt Flicker settle on my shoulder. He curled his tail around my neck and blew a warm breath across my cheek. His scales flickered and glowed. And I thought maybe things would be OK after all.

Maybe we could find a way to keep the dragons. Maybe we would even find out where they called home. After all, I had the map now; perhaps there was more Elvi had to tell us than just how much ash to use. And maybe we'd tackle Liam and his super-sizing dragon in the process.

OK—there were a lot of maybes. With the odd perhaps sprinkled in for good measure.

But here's what I'd realized: Flicker didn't just

shine with bright colors, he shone with bright ideas, too. Like a lightning bolt in the middle of a storm. A beacon, lighting the way. Together, I felt sure we would be prepared for anything.

Well, that's what I thought anyway. But of course, this isn't the end of the story. Not by a long shot.

Acknowledgments

So here come the thank yous, part two!

Huge thanks to Sara Ogilvie for her stunning illustrations. They are simply a joy.

I also want to give a massive thank you to the wonderful people at Piccadilly Press and Bonnier Zaffre for showing so much love and excitement for the series.

To my lovely editors—Georgia Murray, who has brought so much to these books, and Talya Baker, for her eagle-eyed expertise. You have both made this whole process great fun.

To Emma Matthewson for bringing the idea to the Piccadilly team in the first place and to Jane Harris for making my dragons and me feel so at home.

Massive thanks to Nick Stearn, whose cover design and vision for these books, along with Sara's wonderful artwork, has made all three of them so beautiful. And to Sue Michniewicz for her care and creativity with the internal design and layout—you have all made these books look amazing, thank you!

As Tomas might say, mega-tastic thanks to James Horobin, Nico Poilblanc, and the whole sales team who have championed Tomas and the dragons from the very start; Ruth Logan, Ilaria Tarasconi, and Angie Willocks for their hard work in getting these books out into the wider world; Nicola Chapman and Tina Mories for their efforts with the marketing and PR; Heather Featherstone for expert proofreading and Jamie Taylor for organizing the paper and printing and arranging things with the lovely folks at Clays the printers, who welcomed me in to see *The Boy Who Grew Dragons* flying off the press.

A big shout-out to all my new bookish friends—an unexpected and brilliant part of writing has been meeting such amazing people. You're an inspiring bunch!

Special thanks to Polly Faber, Lorraine Gregory, Maz Evans, Ross Montgomery, and Kiran Millwood Hargrave for reading my debut before it was even properly in the world and for their lovely comments about it. Also to James Nicol, Vashti Hardy, Jen Killick, and my writing twin, Tizzie Frankish. You have all been generous to a fault with advice and support. Thank you for making this whole mad malarkey so much fun.

There are some writers who genuinely inspire you to keep going—I'm grateful to Caroline Green, Abi Elphinstone, and SF Said for their advice and honesty along the way.

An extra-special thank you to the book bloggers and reviewers who work so hard to share their love of books with a wider audience. Especially the mighty Jo Clarke—Jo, your excitement for books is infectious! Thanks for all your enthusiasm and support over the past couple of years—and the laughs; you really do keep me grinning!

Similarly to another Jo—my super-agent Jo Williamson.

Finally, to Ian, my rock through everything. And Ben and Jonas—my wonderful boys. Thank you for bringing magic to my everyday.

Andy Shepherd is a children's writer working on middle-grade fiction and picture books. She lives near Cambridge with her husband, two sons, and their Border collie. She spends her spare time trying to figure out how to move this beautiful city closer to the sea. *The Boy Who Lived with Dragons* is her second book. You can follow her on Twitter @andyjshepherd or Facebook at andyshepherdwriter.com.

Sara Ogilvie is an award-winning artist/illustrator. She was born in Edinburgh and now lives in Newcastle upon Tyne. Sara's many picture books include *The Detective Dog* by Julia Donaldson, *The Worst Princess* by Anna Kemp, and *Izzy Gizmo* by Pip Jones. Her middle-grade fiction includes Phil Earle's *Demolition Dad* and others in the Storey Street series.

saraogilvie.com

nbillustration.co.uk/portfolios/sara-ogilv